Vengeful

Out of the Box, Book 6

Robert J. Crane

Vengeful
Out of the Box #6
Robert J. Crane
Copyright © 2015 Midian Press
All Rights Reserved.

1st Edition

1

Sienna

I stood over the grave and stared at the curving letters carved into the stone. The way they were written made the name look elegant. The stone itself was flecked with grey and black, like a rock that couldn't quite decide what color it wanted to be. A hard wind blew past me, stirring my dark hair and blowing strands in my face. I reached up and brushed them away, let them fly behind my head out of sight so I could stare at the grave.

"This is all my fault," I whispered, but it was lost to the wind.

It had been months since he'd died, and the ground was covered over with snow. A cloudy ceiling hung overhead, dark grey that made the tombstone seem like gleaming ivory marble by comparison. I sniffed the air, caught the hard bite of winter as it slipped like a knife through my nasal passages and into my lungs. It cut me like the thought of him being gone, deep inside. I wanted to simply let the stiffness out of the knees I was barely standing on, wanted to fall to the cold, ice-covered earth, to curl up and wrap my coat around myself as I lay there, as close to him as I could get, until the Minnesota skies opened up once more and let fall the snow that would bury me in my final resting place as surely as it had buried him.

It was the chill and misery that made me feel right at home, really. This was exactly the right sort of day for mourning, for stewing. Brooding would not have been out of line. And it was the first time since he'd died that I'd visited his grave.

That I'd had the courage to visit his grave.

"I wanted to avenge you," I said, but the words sounded hollow, like I lacked any feeling to put into them. I probably didn't have any left at this point. My hair whipped in front of my face again, and this time I didn't try to stop it from tickling my forehead as I stared at the marble stone jutting out of the white earth. "I wanted to make it right."

You don't need to, he said from within me.

I looked up at the name carved into the stone, at the curving letters that spelled out *Zachary Sheridan Davis*. I tried to blink back tears, but they came anyway, chilling as they ran down my frigid cheeks.

"He wouldn't have wanted you to do it," a voice came from behind me. I turned, even though I knew who it was. He was tall, my brother. His hair was long and dark and flowed over his shoulders like he used three bottles of conditioner per day. "He could probably tell you himself, though, I guess," Reed said to me, hands stuffed into his black overcoat's pockets.

"He wouldn't be dead if it hadn't been for me," I said, my feet crunching on the snow as I turned to face him, my steps lethargic. It was a half-shuffle, as lifeless as the trees that stood around the graveyard.

"He wouldn't be dead if it hadn't been for Erich Winter," Reed said softly, stepping closer, his footsteps in the snow sounding the inevitable. I couldn't stay here, after all. I had things to do, battles to fight, a war to win. "You can't blame yourself for the act of a madman."

"You'd be surprised what I can blame myself for," I said, looking back at the grave, still and alone on an early Sunday morning. We'd spent Sunday mornings together when he was alive, sleeping in. Playing tug-of-war with the covers on autumn mornings, him careful not to touch my skin for longer than a touch, a caress, watching a movie on Netflix while we stole glances at the sun rising higher in the sky out my balcony window—

The thought of a thousand more Sundays without him knifed into me, stole my breath for a moment. Reed's eyes caught the small motion, and he flinched ever so slightly. "Don't think about it like that."

"I'll think about it however I damned well please," I said. I felt my cheeks flush, and not from the cold this time. They ran hot, like someone had poured scalding water out of my tear ducts. "He didn't die in his bed of old age, okay? He was taken from me, taken by people—"

"Most of whom you've killed," Reed said softly, without any judgment.

"The architect of which is left," I said, sniffing, taking in cold air as my nose started to run. "He's still out there. Still … He got away with it, Reed. And it … it burns."

"You're in a unique position," Reed said, watching me carefully, as though he were afraid to lean in, to grab me in his embrace, to give me a big hug. Most people were afraid of that, really, given what my mere touch could do. But this time, I wanted him to. I needed somebody to, needed someone to fill the space that Zack had occupied, to just … be the person to give me a hug every now and again, to put their arms around me so I could feel the warmth of another human being and realize that I wasn't alone. "You can actually hear the voice of your lost loved one, and I bet—if I know Zack—he doesn't want you to go chasing after the man that killed him."

I don't, you know.

"You have no idea," I said, pretending I couldn't hear the voice within, pretending Reed didn't know what he was talking about. "I may have other things on my plate right now, but if Erich Winter crosses my path, I'm still going to kill him."

There was no mistaking the sadness in Reed's eyes at my pronouncement. "I know."

"Good," I said, wiping my eyes with the cold, rough sleeve of my coat. I turned and looked back at the headstone with its flecks of grey and black, and felt the cold of the season, the grey blanket of the skies settle over me like a strange comfort.

"But if you do this," Reed said, charging on, heedless of my feelings and pissing me off with every syllable, "you know you'll become the kind of person Winter wanted you to be all along."

I steamed where I stood, practically able to feel the heat rising off my forehead, like I had the world's highest-running fever. I kept my eyes anchored on the grave stone, stared at the curve of Zack's name written across it, and when I'd finally composed myself to make my counter-argument without yelling loud enough to wake the dead, I rounded on him—

And he was gone. My shoulders fell, the tension bleeding out as the fight I'd expected failed to emerge. A set of footprints in the snow was the only thing to mark the passage of my brother, my silent guardian, as he left alone with my grief. I stood there for a while, the cold wind ripping into me as I faced the direction my brother had gone, up over the hill, wondering if I should follow after him or simply stay where I was and mourn for a while.

2.

Five Years Later

There was fire all around me, an oven of heat and flame rolling up the leather and plastic coverings to the doors of my brother's Dodge Challenger, blackening the inside of the window glass. My skin charred and melted, the conflagration sweeping up to envelope me where I sat in the passenger seat, the fire moving so fast I didn't even have time to think how to respond.

My thoughts were sluggish from days of being drugged, of being in a forced coma, from having emotions of guilt and horror forced on me. I blinked in the flame as a wave of explosive force rolled over my body, rippling my skin and jarring my internal organs. Standing across a field from the destruction of my brother's car, I probably wouldn't even have felt the force of the bomb going off. Here, it was like firing a shotgun into a lead-lined coffee can. The force rippled around and blew the door off next to me. Bones broke within me, organs ruptured, and skin split open even as it burned.

And dimly, through it all, my mind barely held on to consciousness with the tenacity of a … Wolfe.

Sienna! he shouted in my ear. The flames danced across raw nerve endings, searing my skin off. I lifted my hand and watched it blacken as my eyes burned from the smoke and fire. Then the skin on my fingers grew back like a fast-spreading fungus, like a creepy virus from a sci-fi movie. I watched it happen dully, barely aware, not sure what was going on—

Sienna! Aleksandr Gavrikov cried, and flame surged toward my fingers like I had a magnet for fire, a vacuum to take it all in. I felt powerless in my own body, barely awake, and seeing flame pulled into me like it was drawn to a gravity well under my skin was like an alarm clock for the ages, sending a message to my mind that *Oh dear God it's time to wake up—*

I snapped out of it and panic rushed through me. I was in a burning car, fresh air feeding the fire from where the door next to me had been blown off, cool night so buried under flame and heat that I couldn't even feel it. Or maybe it was because my skin was burning and being regrown in the space of seconds, my nerve endings flash-fried and regenerated by the power of Wolfe as I watched them go and come like a child staring stupidly at a car barreling down the street at him.

SIENNA! Zack shouted at me from within my own mind.

I pushed my hands forward and tugged at Gavrikov in my mind. His relief at my awakening surged into the back of my head, and I sensed the fire rush harder toward me. I drew it in without worrying about just my hands. I opened my mouth and breathed in flame like a dragon in reverse, tearing it out of the air in front of me and letting it diffuse through my very flesh, drawn off and siphoned off and dispersed into my body. My clothes burned and added the black stench of their smoke to the interior of the car as the fire began to subside. I pulled the heat out of the air and dragged the inferno out of the dashboard, the engine, the fuel tank, pulling it all to me. It was like taking the deepest breath you could imagine, filling your lungs full to capacity and then drawing in more without letting out any of what you'd already gotten.

And then, just when I felt as though I were completely full, I realized it was done.

I sagged against the melted slag that was my seat. I exhaled and black smoke came out of my mouth like a factory chimney. I coughed and spit out cinders, ash running down my already scorched chin. Every nerve in my body screamed with the pain as I regrew my flesh, tender and new. My mouth tasted disgusting, like ashtray mixed with meatloaf and bad coffee, brewed in a chamber pot for six months before someone poured it down my gullet. I gagged but held it together, my neck sagging against the seat. Hard, hot metal jutted out and poked into my back, and my head rolled with the exhaustion that had settled over me. I didn't feel like I could even move enough to the side to fall out of the car—

Then my eyes settled on the man in the driver's seat, and I felt sick in a whole new way.

Oh—

Oh no—

Not—

"Reed," I breathed, my throat scratchy like I'd dragged a barbed wire feeding tube up it. "Reed." I couldn't muster an exclamation point, not with the amount of carcinogens I had just consumed, like a chain-smoker who went through eight cartons an hour. I fumbled, raising a hand, trying to reach him—

His skin was black, and where it wasn't, blisters were already bubbled up like space domes on a faraway moon, marking every crater. His eyes were closed, his long, dark air grey with ash. His clothing was black and peeled and barely any of it was still there. His belt buckle shone in the light of a nearby lamp.

I tried again to reach my brother, stretching my hand out across the charred remains of the center console between us. My fingers shook as I extended my arm, like I'd had a lifetime of exertions today already, like my muscles were weak from atrophy. I stretched my blackened, soot-covered hand toward him, and I landed it on his cheek.

He did not stir, did not move, save for a thin trickle of red blood that ran down his face to his chin. My arm lost all power and I dropped it hard against the scorched leather. I could see dim shapes moving outside his door—which was gone—and the only thought I could muster was that I hoped it was help that was on the way before I dropped into a darkness as complete as a silent winter night.

3.

Ma

"Damn, girl," Claudette "Ma" Clary said, looking at the dancing flames on the widescreen TV as they glowed white and phosphorescent from the surveillance camera footage, "you didn't just stick your head into an Easy-Bake Oven this time." She looked at Cassidy Ellis, all pale skin and gangly limbs, dripping water from that wetsuit contraption she wore into her sensory deprivation tank. Claudette knew pride when she saw it, and it was all over that girl's face, flushed pink where normally it was snowy white, and she knew she would have to let a little of the air out of the girl's sense of accomplishment. But it needed to happen, she consoled herself, because this—this idea, done without anyone else's approval—this was damned crazy, and it could just about wreck them all if it came falling down like a car coming off the hydraulic lift.

"I thought it was a good, fast reaction to our last plan falling apart," Cassidy said, and she puffed up with a little hint of defiance, digging in to defend her plan. "I hired the assassin and had the bomb in place within minutes of—"

"You didn't kill her," Junior said, staring at the screen. It drew everyone's attention back for a minute, watching figures running up. They were pulling Sienna Nealon and her brother out of the flaming wreck of the vehicle, all twisted from the force of the explosion, the chassis exposed. There wasn't much that was obvious on the grainy surveillance video, but Sienna Nealon spitting black smoke out of her lungs was pretty easy to see. And cause for some concern for Ma. "And you wrecked a damned pretty car in the process," Junior almost whimpered. "I mean, I'm okay with killing people, but wrecking a brand new Dodge Challenger like that is just a sin against nature."

"Maybe we should keep our eye on the prize," Eric Simmons said. Ma watched him out of the corner of her eye. He had a hand over his mouth, tentative-like. She hadn't known him for but a few months, but she'd seen enough to know the game he was running on Cassidy. She was sure Simmons would defend his little girlfriend; he knew he'd have to in order to keep the girl from having one of her little fits. Ma had spied a couple cracks in that relationship and knew a little leverage would pop it apart easily, but for now, she let him do his thing, keep his ass out of that particular fire. "The drug we arranged … that was supposed to kill Sienna. Painfully. So …"

"So why's she popping her not-so-pretty face out of a car after sucking out all the fire like she just went down on a—" That was Denise, and Ma cuffed her right across the back of the head, stopping her before she could finish her dirty, profane thought. "Owww." Denise rubbed the spot on her crown where Ma had got her, looking up resentfully.

"That plan clearly didn't work," Ma said, trying to move the discussion along.

"Neither did sending Anselmo after Reed Treston," Cassidy said, looking Ma in the eyes only for a second. If there was one thing that drove Ma nuts about that girl, it was that she couldn't even look a body in the eye for a few seconds. Just slyly looked at you and then looked away, like it was some sort of physical imposition to try and make eye contact. Ma judged her some sort of coward for that, maybe like a rodent. A wet one at that, one that climbed out of the nearest toilet and scampered around the house, constantly underfoot.

"I did that to get rid of Anselmo," Ma said, shrugging. "I make no bones about it. The man was trouble, and I didn't want him in my house. He didn't want to be here, so it seemed like a natural fit to set him loose on the Treston boy."

"Anselmo was really useful," Simmons said, still hiding his disappointment behind the hand in front of his mouth. Someone had told Ma once that people who spoke from behind their hand were liars. Looking at Simmons, she believed it. What amazed her was that Cassidy bought her boyfriend's lies hook, line and sinker, like a widemouth bass on a good lure. She had all the power of technology at her fingertips, and she never once used it to expose herself to the obvious truths sitting right in front of her. The girl was brilliant, too, easily the book-smartest person Ma had ever run across. But she lacked the common sense God gave a garden snake, which was why Eric Simmons had her wrapped around his thin, earth-shaking, sissy-manicured little fingers.

"He was a bomb ready to go off any time," Ma said with some force, yanking that carpet out from under Simmons without worrying about it giving him a burn on his soft, probably-lotioned face. There was a flash of anger in Simmons's eyes, but he held it back. He didn't like it here; that was obvious to anyone, but by now Ma knew that he specifically didn't like her or any of her clan, either. The feeling was more or less mutual, too, and that city-slickin' son of a bitch could go back to LA or New York or wherever the hell he wanted to be for all she cared.

After she was done using him, anyway.

"We're still down a team member," Simmons said, recovering. "And now we've got no plan."

"Plus," Denise said, making that face she always did that turned her ugly as sin, "now Sienna Nealon's gonna be mad as hell when she wakes up, because we done killed her brother—"

"He's still alive," Cassidy said, a little meekly, drawing every eye in the room. *Of course she didn't mention this before she started showing us the video of her little "triumph."* "I was thinking about—"

"Don't," Ma said calmly. "Don't lose focus on what's important here, and it ain't her stupid brother. That was Anselmo's grudge, not ours. I got no grievance with that boy."

"Odds are good he's gonna have one with us, now," Junior said, looking a little pensive as the security camera footage looped on the widescreen again. He was watching it closer than a football game. He cringed when the car blew up, mouth a jagged line of genuine pain, and she knew it wasn't because of what happened to the people inside.

"He's in the hospital," Cassidy said. "All it would take is a dose of poison—"

"Will you just lay off it already?" Ma turned her eyes on the girl. "Don't we have a big enough problem to deal with already? Is your head so far up your own damned disk drive you don't see what's coming?"

Cassidy looked chastened, blinking away from Ma's hard gaze. "No one uses disk drives anymore," she said sulkily.

Ma ignored her. "Have you seen what happens when Sienna Nealon gets mad? When she goes whole hog on someone she's pissed off at?"

"She doesn't have a clue who we are," Cassidy said, blushing a little. She looked at Ma for almost a second before she blinked away, but Ma could see her digging in again. "She doesn't know where we are—"

"You think that'll stop her?" Ma asked, folding her big forearms one over the other. "I hate to be the bearer of bad news for you, but that girl ain't got an ounce of quit, and when her back's up, she ain't gonna stop 'til she's done." She glanced at Junior and Denise. "We know that by hard experience."

Cassidy blinked, processing it all. "Because of your son, you mean."

Ma didn't look away from her. She knew full well that the girl didn't mean anything by it; she just didn't feel on the same level as a normal human being. It was all detached to her, like a garage way far from the house, maybe on an adjacent plot of land. "Because of that, yeah. She killed him, him and the others that she thought wronged her—"

"She stalked 'em like a deer in gun season," Junior threw in, looking a little pissy.

"Drowned him," Denise said, wearing a little fury of her own on her sleeve. "Cold-hearted bitch."

"This was supposed to be a quiet thing," Ma said. "We weren't supposed to drag family into it because that's the fastest way to a feud. It was supposed to be silent— poisoning, a bullet in the night, something fast, over. Now you got us in on bombs and explosions—the law's gonna get involved, no way around that now, and who knows where it's going to lead? Well, if it comes to our door, I can tell you right now, I—ain't—gonna—be—happy." She said the last with the hardest edge of all, and she knew how to do it. She'd raised Claude, after all, and then Junior and Denise after, and they may have been a rowdy, mischievous bunch, but they knew not to raise her hackles.

Cassidy looked appropriately cowed. "I'm sorry," she said, muffled. Her neckline was all red like someone had slapped the skin there hard.

"Well, what are we gonna do now?" Ma asked, ready to move on. She didn't forgive and forget, she just forgave. Didn't do any good to keep turning it over again and again when it was plain the girl just didn't know squat about people. Brilliant mind, probably could get a PhD in nuclear physics in a couple of months, but she just lacked where it counted. She'd probably starve to death in the middle of a Wal-Mart.

"I can work our press contacts," Cassidy said, raising her eyes again. "Raise the heat level, get them fishing on this story, make it ... uncomfortable for her to go back to work."

"She's still suspended, ain't she?" Junior asked, looking around. "Because of that last paparazzi we put on her?"

"I think it's coming time to cut the ties," Ma said. "I'm getting worried enough that her dying painfully ain't as important to me as her just being dead at this point." She worked at a piece of corn stuck in her teeth. "How about we get on that?"

"How do you want to do it?" Denise asked, and she sounded almost hungry.

"Like putting an animal out of its misery," Ma said, and she caught a flash of surprise from Simmons. He was such a weak-titted little princess. "No warning, no time to scream or even realize what's coming ... just done." She worked that kernel loose and spit it out. She'd vacuum it up later. "Let's just be done with her already before this gets any more out of hand."

4.

Sienna

I woke up screaming, my back wet from sweat or something else, my hand finding cold steel on either side of me in the form of bed railings. I sat up, a thin white sheet tangled around me as I stared into the dim light of the infirmary. A light clicked on and I had to shut my eyes quickly in order to keep it from overwhelming me.

"Whoa, there," came the calm voice of Dr. Quinton Zollers. I opened my eyes to see him staring down at me, warm eyes and mocha skin, and for once it did little to soothe me. He brushed my arm with a careful hand, and even the flesh-to-flesh contact did nothing to calm me down.

"Chill, Sienna," Scott Byerly said, appearing opposite Zollers. His face was redder than usual, cheeks all flushed like he'd been on a long run, or just gotten back from the gym. His normally curly hair hung sweaty, clumped, like he'd just stepped out of the shower.

"We're here," Ariadne Fraser said from the end of the bed, stepping into view as I sat there, bolt upright, every muscle tense enough to jump out of my own skin. The air carried a scorched smell mixed with wetness, and I realized that the mattress upon which I was laying had a more than small moisture problem.

"Well, not all of us are," Augustus Coleman said from

somewhere over Ariadne's shoulder. I angled to try and see him, his face obscured by Dr. Zoller's body, and the doc moved aside to oblige me, giving a glimpse of a dark-skinned young man flat on his back in a cervical collar, IV resting at his side. His eyes blinked slowly, exaggerated, and I knew he was still drugged from the night before. Everyone turned their head to look at him, and I caught the accusation from Scott and Ariadne. "What? We gonna to lie to her now?"

"Don't lie," I said, voice low and throaty, yet not remotely sexy. More like I was out of breath, which I was. I coughed and tasted the acrid aroma of the smoke I'd inhaled while breathing in the fire. "Not now." I turned my head to look at Dr. Zollers. "Where's Reed?"

I saw the hesitation before he answered. "He's in Methodist Hospital."

I pulled my arm away from him. "I need to go."

"Sienna," Scott said, leaning over me, "you were just in a car that was blown up underneath you—"

"I'm fine, thanks," I said, looking to see if there were any IVs I needed to rip out before I got up. There weren't, not a hint of them, and I realized the other presence that was missing from the room—Dr. Isabella Perugini. There was no sign of her dark hair and even darker countenance, of her white lab coat trolling its way through the wrecked and sodden infirmary with a black cloud over her head. I knew in an instant where she was, where she had to be given the circumstances.

"Sienna—" Ariadne started.

"Not now," I said and slid down the wet mattress. I heard water rushing out of it under my weight as I moved, a reminder of what had happened in this infirmary only hours earlier. I skirted the edge of the bed railing and Zollers did not move to stop me. He wouldn't have been quick enough to in any case, but from the way I saw him standing there, silent, reserved, I knew he'd opted to pick his battles and that this wasn't one he was prepared to fight.

"You can't just run off—" Ariadne said.

"I won't." I slid out of bed, looking down at the hospital gown that was draped over me in lieu of my burned clothes. I didn't even care at this point, not even a little.

"Bad wording, Ariadne," Augustus said, continuing his role as drug-addled comic relief. "Now watch her fl—"

Gavrikov, I thought, projecting the words deep inside. It was second nature by now, and Aleksandr Gavrikov, probably sensing that I was in NO MOOD, meekly complied. Gravity cut out beneath me and my feet lifted off the ground. I floated a foot in the air for a moment and then took control, leaving all their protestations behind as I flew out of the infirmary, my hospital gown flapping behind me, threatening to rip off from the wind shear as I blew out of the doors of headquarters and past the scorched wreckage of the Dodge Challenger parked just outside.

5.

I pushed into my brother's hospital room past the three security guards and eight of our own agents posted in the hall, ignoring their doubtful expressions. No one said anything, presumably because the look on my face and my attire told them everything they needed to know about how I'd take any attempt to slow me down. After all, it wasn't much of a secret among our own people that only a few hours ago I'd been a human bomb about to go off.

The hospital room was small, with dull beige walls and aged tile floors like every other hospital I'd ever been in. The smell was antiseptic, and the sound of a respirator hissed in the quiet night under the sound of the beeping heartbeat monitor.

Dr. Isabella Perugini looked over her shoulder at me, her long, black hair pulled back in a ponytail that made her look somehow more severe. She wore no makeup, not that she needed much of it to begin with, but the lack of it left her looking a little faded—unless it was the stress that had done that. Her eyes didn't look puffy at all, just tired, thinly lidded, and she only looked at me for a second before she turned back to the bed, one hand resting at the base of her neck and the other folded around her midsection.

I eased up to the edge of the bed and got a good first look at my brother. His skin was still charred and broiled, blistered in some places and peeling in others. There were a few spots where angry red skin hinted at only first-degree burns. They were few and far between, however. "Hey," I mumbled as I stood there at her side.

She didn't look at me. "You are all right, then." She said it, didn't ask, because after being my doctor for oh-so-many years, she just knew.

"I am," I said, regardless of the fact that we were both fully aware of my near-invincibility. I moved on from the comfortable to the question neither of us wanted to ask. "How's he doing?"

"Burns over ninety-nine percent of his body," she said, as tonelessly as if she were delivering news about a patient she barely knew, not a man she'd been sleeping with for over three years.

"But he'll heal," I said, taking a breath of relief.

"Possibly," she said, and here I caught the first hint of something wrong. "These were not third-degree burns ... they stretched deep beneath the epidermis into the subcutaneous layer." She swallowed visibly, and her hand clutched tighter at her throat, as though she were choking on the words she was trying to get out. "There are ... complications. Inhalation—"

"Is he going to live?" I asked, cutting right to the quick.

She turned her head to look at me, and I saw a woman who didn't honestly know the answer to the question. "I am not sure."

That one hit me right where it hurt. My stomach dropped like someone had just hit it and used a sledgehammer to do the job. I leaned against the bottom edge of his bed, felt the pressed wood crumple under my unexpected strength. I sucked in a deep breath like I had to fight to get it back, which I did. It felt a little like I'd been hit in the gut, hard, like I'd dropped out of the sky and landed belly button first on a flagpole. Which I had done, once, when I was still learning to fly. It hurts about as much as you'd expect.

"The next twenty-four hours will be the most crucial,"

she said, back to playing the role of the cool doctor and shutting off the fiery Italian lover like she was twisting a valve.

"Okay," I said, because I didn't know what else to say.

We stood in silence for a while, maybe minutes, maybe hours, it was tough for me to tell. I got lost in a memory, the reminder of how Reed had approached me the first time I'd visited Zack's grave, after—

Well, after.

"Do you know who did this?" Dr. Perugini asked, still fixed on Reed, standing in the middle of her damned domain, the medical world, and looking as helpless as I was.

"No," I said, "but I can guess. Eric Simmons. His little friend the Brain. They're the ones with the grudge—"

"What are you going to do about it?" she asked, and her hand moved like she wanted to touch him, but she held back.

"I think you can guess."

Her fingers returned uselessly to the base of her throat. "He wouldn't want that."

"He wouldn't want me to catch who's responsible?" I gave her one of those sidelong glances that they make internet memes out of, my best, *Oh, you're just an idiot* look.

"He wouldn't want you to go after them furious," she said.

I listened to her words, read her movement. "You don't mind, though, do you?" She tensed only slightly, and I asked a really stupid question that I was sure I already knew the answer to. "This is my fault, isn't it?"

She tilted her head to look at me as she answered, and she looked ... thoughtful. "I don't think so."

I blinked in utter surprise. "No?" I'd been ready for her to whirl on me, to start hurling insults and accusations right in my face, to let loose that full head of Dr. Perugini steam that she'd unleashed on more occasions than I could count. I wanted her to do it, to have my brother's lover fuel my internal fury. I could feel it boiling inside, the guilt and the rage, looking for an outlet, already on the stove. I wanted someone else to stoke the flames, the give me that last push by making me complicit.

"I don't blame you," she said finally.

"Why the hell not?" I smacked dry lips together after forcing the question out of my mouth.

"You want to feel bad," she said, nodding without looking at me. "Wronged. I don't have it in me to do this thing for you, and he wouldn't want me to anyway." Now she looked at me and quivered. "I'm not angry at you. I don't blame you … I'm too busy being scared for him."

I staggered back, taking it harder than if she'd struck me, than if she'd grabbed the IV tree and impaled me on the end. I felt so weak, so tired, so out of sorts that the world around me was starting to feel surreal in its wrongness. She watched me stumble back with something akin to concern, maybe the closest to it I'd ever seen from her when aimed at me. "Are you—?"

I didn't even give her time to finish the question. I took a last look at my brother, burned almost beyond recognition, breathing with the aid of a machine, and I ran from the room. I ignored the agents who asked me if I was all right, paid no attention to security, and stumbled straight to the window at the end of the hall, breaking through the glass and leaping out into the night with my hospital gown flapping behind me, possibly more wounded than if Isabella Perugini had attacked me with everything she had.

6.

By the time I got back to the agency, I was calm enough to stop off at my quarters to change into some clothes, to dump some kibble in a dish for the dog, then fly to the roof of HQ, calm enough not to Kool-Aid-Man my way through the fourth-floor windows. I descended the stairs like a human being, resolving to hold together even though I really didn't want to adult right now. I wanted to scream like a toddler who just lost a juice box, wanted to go to sleep and wake up a year from now. Or a year before now.

I had many powers, but those weren't in my set, unfortunately, so instead I went to go see a man about people I could vent my rage on.

The fourth-floor lights were on in a few places, but I could tell pretty much no one was home. It was somewhere near five in the morning, I reckoned, and the entire agency had been in manhunt mode the last few days. Since the manhunt had been resolved hours ago, that meant everyone was crashed out at their homes, probably.

Probably.

I checked his cubicle first, and when I didn't find him there but saw the computer was still running a compiling program, I knew he was nearby. I floated into the air and did a three-sixty of the entire floor until I found a conference room with its door shut. I shot across the massive open space, blasting about ten thousand pieces of paper into a storm behind me and putting the lie to Director Andrew Phillips's 'paperless office' policy.

I similarly managed not to burst through the door of the conference room, or the wall, but only by using some of that vanishingly small amount of restraint I carried with me almost nowhere. I opened the door without concern for its occupant, and I was standing over him before he had a chance to realize there was a presence in the room and that it was a human being inches from his nose. He'd set his thick-framed glasses on the table. I snatched them up and jammed them onto his face so I wouldn't have to wait through that step.

His eyelids fluttered, slightly exaggerated by the thickness of his lenses, the fluorescent lights from outside spilling into the conference room. His dark hair was flattened in the back from leaning against the chair he was sleeping in. When J.J. did finally open his eyes—and keep them open this time—it didn't take more than a couple flutters for him to realize that shit just got real.

"Oh, f—" he said as he tried to sit up abruptly. It was a doomed maneuver, and he started to topple back in his chair. I, however, was prepared for this and lifted him by his lapels into the air with me as the chair came crashing down on the conference room floor. It had a five-point base, supposedly making it harder to overturn in the name of idiot-proofing. Clearly, the designers had never met idiots of the sort I had to deal with.

I carried him by his lapels through the air as he struggled instinctively against my mother-bird grip on him. "What are you doing?" he managed to cry out by the time I was halfway back to his cubicle.

"I need you to work," I said, drifting down and dropping him into his own chair.

He hit gracelessly, spinning it halfway around thanks to his flailing limbs, nearly overturning this one as well. *You had one job, J.J.* "Have you thought about just asking—like a normal person would?!"

"Do I strike you as a normal person?" I let gravity reassert its dominion over me and thumped to the ground feet-first, landing like a badass.

"I hope you're not going to hit me at all," he said, fiddling with his glasses.

I looked him straight in the eye. "Let's skip the threats. The explosion."

"Yeah," he said, looking sort of like he was returning to business mode, though giving me a wary look. "Figured you'd be in about that. Let me tell you, that going off outside the window was actually a little more gentle than what you just did. Just for future reference."

"Information," I said.

"Manners," he replied, and I got right up in his face, causing him to squirm. "I can see you're ... uh ... strained at the moment, and not of the 're' variety, so why don't I just ..." He tapped on his keyboard while turning to give me a close-up view of his cheek. I just kept right there, like I was going to Hannibal Lecter him and take a bite if he pissed me off. "Here we go."

I pulled back enough to get the stink of cat out of my nostrils and so I could see his monitor. "What the hell is this?"

"These are email accounts tied to IP addresses of your much-vaunted 'Brain' villain," J.J. said, apparently deciding to wisely forgo any additional unamusing witticisms in favor of extending his life expectancy. "I caught them last episode, while we were dealing with Anselmo and Bryant Cunningham. They've been waging a PR war against you, tipping off reporters to all sorts of stuff that's ... well—"

"They've been messing with my public image," I said, adding that fuel to the fire that was burning not-so-deep inside of me. "She's been upping the speed on the treadmill as I try to outrun these media shitstorms."

"Bad analogy," he said, shaking his head, "there's not a

treadmill out there that you couldn't outrun 'til it smoked—"
He caught the look on my face and stopped. "Yes. Right. So
... these are the Brain's emails ... and this is what went out
early this morning, while I was sleeping."

He punched a key and brought up a wall of text, six
emails in a chain with replies and everything. I blinked as I
scanned, and my blood grew colder and colder. "Who the
hell is the recipient?"

J.J. smacked his lips together. "Local assassin, near as I
can tell. He doesn't have a file with Homeland Security or the
FBI, which means—"

"He's good," I said, feeling that chill settle over my bones
as I kept reading. "How do I find him?"

"His name's Michael Shafer, and he communicates over a
VPN that's technically untraceable—" J.J. froze mid-
sentence, looking at me like I was going to smack him. "You
know what? I don't want to waste your time with the
technicals—"

"Good call."

"Anyway, I already found him." He tapped the keyboard
a few times and an address popped up along with a Google
map. "Sending to your phone."

I heard a chirrup and pulled out my phone to find the
map already there. I stared at it for only a second, the
thought I had not really a thought, just a generalized urge to
head straight for my enemy. "Okay," I said and waited for
him to say something—a wiseass comment, a word of
caution, anything. He didn't, he just sat there looking down,
like his lap was the most interesting thing in the world. So ...
like any other man, really.

With nothing and no one to stop me, I turned and flew
back to the stairwell, erupting out of the roof door and into
the night.

7.

I went cannonballing into a house right on the shores of Lake Minnetonka without worrying about how much I was probably lowering the property values just by being there. I burst through a full plate-glass window, not for the first time that night, using Wolfe to heal the massive lacerations I suffered before I bled all over the place. Shards of glass landed all over the floor and I startled the shit out of the guy who had been walking across the far side of the luxuriously appointed living room with a big ol' snifter of brandy in his hand, a spotted maroon bathrobe knotted around his waist.

Everything about this guy screamed EXPENSIVE, including the diamond-crusted ring on his index finger, his carefully sculpted grey-tinged hair, parted on the side and sweeping back, and his fuzzy slippers. Wool or something, I think. They looked comfy.

"Hi," I said, not in a friendly way, hovering rather ominously over his lushly appointed cream-colored couch. He didn't even have a TV in this room, just a bar cabinet, tons of wood shelving with books, and furniture that looked like it didn't come cheap. All that and a full view of Lake Minnetonka by moonlight. I glanced down and saw a Persian rug that probably cost more than I made in a year.

"Good God," he said, ducking his head and raising his hands, apparently a little surprised that I'd just burst into his living room while he was having his nightcap.

"Not quite," I said. His eyes were fixed on mine, and his mouth was only slightly agape. "God forgives, I'm told. Me? Not so much." I stole another glance around the room, feeling like I needed slightly more from him before I commenced to pounding him into sausage meat. Probably very luxurious sausage meat, but still. "So … crime pays, huh?"

"Very well, actually," he said, his brain apparently not getting the memo that when you're in over your head, you should shut your mouth. Instead, he took a couple steps toward his liquor cabinet and opened a bottle on the top, taking his time, pouring another for himself. I suspected he needed it after the start I'd just given him. He pointed to a second snifter and shrugged when he caught the look on my face. "How about government service? Is it as bad as everything I've heard?"

Quick on his feet, back to getting a drink and having a casual conversation about the financial benefits of criminality seconds after the world's premiere superheroine burst through his window.

Ding, ding, ding. We have a winner.

I swooped down to get a grip on him so I could take him on a quick night flight/interrogation high up in the air before dropping him like Sokovia on an unsuspecting world. To my surprise, he threw the brandy in my face and dodged left fast enough that I actually had to pause to counter.

And that brandy? It must have been expensive, because it *burned*. All the way down.

It wasn't a little burn, either, it was the kind that made you blind, made your skin smoke. The smell of alcohol was absent, a strong chemical smell heavy in my nose instead. "I wish you hadn't come here," he said, sounding regretful.

I turned on the Gavrikov and Wolfe all at once, felt the burning on my skin halt even as I burst into flames. "You're saying this now, before I even have a chance to really wreck your leather-bound books and eliminate the smell of rich mahogany from your life. Let's see how you feel after I burn this motha to the—"

Whatever he threw on me ignited with a lot more gusto than I'd expected, propelling me backward through a wall and causing me to flip from the force of the explosion. Harsh chemical flame and dust poured into my nasal passages as I crashed through drywall and wood, my body pinwheeling as I spun through the air, inadvertently lighting flame to everything I touched until I came down, hard, and the world went dark around me.

8.

I forced my eyes back open, reflecting not for the first time that in spite of being in something of an induced coma only hours before and an unconscious state not long after, I kinda wanted a nap. Again. Getting my ass kicked really takes it out of me.

I shook my head as I came up, trying to get rid of the bell-ringing effects of that caustic-plus-explosive mix I'd just had thrown into my face, but smoke was streaming into my eyes, nose and mouth, causing me to cough and sputter. I realized I had a hell of a headache, maybe worse than when the car had exploded, and I wondered how long I'd been out, because the bed was already fully engulfed and flames were already creeping up the walls.

Normally, I would have noticed someone pouring an explosive chemical mixture into a brandy snifter from across the room. Something about the smell tended to trip metahuman senses under normal conditions. I could only assume my emotional state was affecting my mad skills. "Well, shit," I said as the smoke started to grow thick around the ceiling. This was not exactly going to plan.

Perhaps caution? Wolfe advised, so out of character I thought it was Roberto Bastian speaking at first.

"Perhaps you should go screw yourself with something sharp," I replied, rising off the fiery mattress and looked to my left. "Give me a few minutes to wrap this up and I'll imagine into your existence something suitably pointy for you to get the job done with." Fire was crawling up the fancy curtains and the smoke they were giving off was messing with my view of the lake, which was starting to show signs of the impending sunrise somewhere off to the east.

He's only trying to help, Eve Kappler said a little resentfully.

"I'm in a burning house and I just got attacked by someone smart enough—or stupid enough—to keep a booze bottle full of flammable liquid in their liquor cabinet in case company like me comes calling," I snapped. "Captain Obvious's advice is not so helpful right now."

Without waiting to hear a reply from my mental spectator gallery, I burst through the wall into the living room, which was not quite in flames yet. It was, however, still covered in broken glass, and empty of Michael Shafer, whom I presently wanted to expose to broken glass, flames, and my fist, not necessarily in that order. Rather than say something to announce myself in case he was lying in wait, I drifted through the air, careful not to make any noise.

Then the smoke alarms started wailing in the room I'd set on fire and put that plan right out the window. I heard the klaxon taken up by every other smoke detector in the house, and that pretty well ruined my ability to hear, like a month full of Rammstein concerts piped directly into my eardrums.

I considered just getting the hell out of the house and letting it burn, swooping into the air and looking down, watching the exits until someone came out, but that didn't really fit my furious and raging emotional state. No, I wasn't the type to sit quietly in wait for someone who'd just ambushed me, because that would be entirely too smart.

Instead, I burst through the wall across from me, smashing into where I assumed the master bedroom would be. I drew hard on Wolfe's healing abilities the whole time, and it turned out I needed them, and badly, because I came crashing through the master bathroom instead and absolutely racked my knee on a marble countertop.

While I was filling the air with anger, flames and swearing (all related), I saw movement through the door to the master bedroom ahead. Reflecting again that perhaps I was going about this thing all wrong (but with more colorful language), I shot ahead like a fiery rocket, watching my orange-colored reflection in the shiny, ivory-colored floor tiles and the mirrors that surrounded the two separate vanities and the enormous glass shower parked in the corner of the room that would have been big enough to clean off a small elephant.

As I flew into the bedroom, someone swung a wooden chair right into my face. It hurt, of course, all the more so because I didn't have Wolfe front of mind at the moment. I felt my cheekbones shatter like a glass dropped off a ten story building, my skin bursting open at the hundred mile an hour impact. My vision cut out and my lower body flipped under the artificial clothesline and rammed into the bed, shattering the baseboard and my back in the process.

This was not anywhere close to my finest hour.

I lay there, stunned, bleeding in a pile, blind save for a very tiny amount of vision in one eye. Blood spurted out of my mouth in a very wet, very nasty cough. The sound of fire alarms wailing around me was nothing compared to the insensate feeling in my own head, my neck at a terrible angle to the rest of my body. Every breath I took was choked with my own bloody spittle, and I must have sounded pathetic as I fought even to get a glimpse of the room around me.

As per usual, it was way nicer than anything of mine.

"What do we do?" I heard Michael Shafer ask. I could tell it was him over the harsh ringing in my ears and the sirens going off. Dimly, I realized that it hadn't even occurred to me that there might be more than one person in the house.

The answer came from a different voice, this one female, and possessed of none of the maternal kindness that people sometimes associate with women. This one was cold, uncaring, and more than a little pissed off. We could have been friends, I like to think, if not for her answer. "We kill her," she said, and the next sound I heard was the click of a trigger being pulled.

9.

A shotgun blast went off right in the back of my head just as I managed to get Wolfe in my mind, ramming my face into the oaken floorboards from the force of the explosive blast of pellets that swarmed my skull. It was like getting stung by a thousand angry gnats at once, like Hellraiser-type pins stabbed into my scalp as the force smashed my face into the floor, all while my body was already broken in about two dozen places and trying to heal.

Best. Night. Ever.

Right about the time my body started to resume its normal shape, I caught a whiff of the panic that was congealing in the air around me. I heard Shafer curse under his breath, probably after his lady friend tried to blow my head off with a shotgun and realized I was impervious. Should have used a handgun, folks. I'd been blasting myself with buckshot of increasingly powerful levels for months all over my body, trying to coarsen my skin when I was in Wolfe mode. Thousands of years of doing similar things to himself had made Wolfe damned near impervious to physical harm before I met him. I hadn't been gutsy enough to progress to shooting myself with full-metal-jacketed bullets yet, but it was on my list of things to do for next year.

I swept a foot out hard in the direction that I suspected my female assailant stood and was rewarded by a sharp cry of pain as I swept her legs. I thrust both palms against the ground as if doing a push up, but used Gavrikov's powers of flight to switch off gravity as I did so. I leapt into the air and flipped, catching Michael Shafer with a stylistically badass kick as I did so. It wasn't my strongest, but it knocked him back a few steps, leaving a dent in the drywall where he hit.

It should have put him through it, which, when coupled with his fast reaction in throwing the snifter at me earlier, told me something about Michael Shafer.

This sonofagun was a metahuman.

I didn't even need to vow that there'd be no more Ms. Nice Lady, I just flew at him with everything I had and smashed him through the wall. He took the hit and rolled as he landed on his nicely manicured lawn below, and I did a quick Yeager loop and drilled him into the earth with a crash-landing punch that would have been a lot sweeter if he hadn't dodged out of some of the impact at the last second.

We were both a half a foot into the ground when we started to come out of the second's worth of stun that followed my landing on him, and I locked eyes with his. He had a pained look on his face, but not as pained as he ought to have looked after I drilled him like I did. I punched him with a sharp jab, the kind that I use to break bulletproof glass, and his head rocked back. When he bobble-headed his way back, it was with none of the blank look or wooziness that he should have had.

Instead the bastard headbutted me right in the nose, and I heard my cartilage break. Warm blood dripped down my upper lip, giving me a red Hitler mustache and pissing me off even more. "So that's how it's going to be?" I hit him again, and again, and again, and again, and—

Well, it went on for a while.

I pounded him right in the kisser, my knuckles bleeding after the second punch from exceeding the force limits a human body is supposed to take. The big secret of metas, of course, is that while we heal faster and are stronger than humans, we're not invulnerable to them, per se. I mean, with

34

Wolfe's power I'm a lot closer, but a normal person could conceivably knock me out with a properly aimed sucker punch. It'd be a frosty day in hell before I'd let anyone close enough to do that, and I'd have to not have Wolfe pulled up in my mind, but it could happen.

As a consequence, my knuckles were splitting open and healing after each punch, the skin not quite accustomed to hammering against something this hard, this repetitively. Blood ran down my wrist, tickling and annoying me, but not as much as the douche canoe I was battering. Most people gave up the damned ghost after a couple punches, but Michael Shafer was still looking at me with not-so-veiled-murder in his eyes after however many punches. He got his mouth open and I saw the glint of his teeth in the light as I went to punch him again. He bit down with perfect timing, right on my already-bloody knuckles, and suddenly I knew just what kind of meta this bastard was.

I forget the official title, but Japanese called them "Iron Tooth." As he ripped my middle and ring fingers off my right hand, my textbook knowledge of this type of meta went beyond the theoretical and well into the range of "Soon To Be a Trophy Head Hanging on My Wall." The way things were going, I'd probably get my own outrage Facebook post to be shared the world over for it. I didn't care; I'd even make sure to shine up his teeth every few days so they didn't lose their luster or get dusty.

Who bites in a fistfight? Honestly.

I didn't stare in horror at my missing fingers like he probably expected me to, because this wasn't my first rodeo of missing body parts. Instead, I pulled clear of him, getting to my feet and beginning to do what I do best.

I kicked him like his belly was a piñata and I was a spoiled, hangry (a portmanteau of hungry-angry, before you try and correct my spelling, you unsophisticates) four year-old with the sweet tooth from hell. If his teeth were iron, I was hoping his belly was a soft pouch, and I stomped and stomped until I felt like even a tortoise with a titanium shell couldn't have survived in his intestines. I hoped he felt like he'd eaten eighty-seven bean burritos and had nary a hope of Gas-X ever, and judging by the way his eyes were bulging out of his head when I got done, I wasn't far off.

Blood was streaming down his lips by the light of the house on fire behind us, and he was cradling his tender underbelly, which was distended inward like he was about two inches from being cut in half. "Smile, you prick," I said, and wound up for the kick, which was going right to his stupid face.

I got dragged down from behind right as my balance was at its worst point, and my shoulders hit dirt, as did my ass. It didn't really hurt, but Shafer used the opportunity to roll over and bite me in the leg. That hurt.

And was also the last straw.

I saw his woman coming at me from above with a kick, and I grabbed her by the ankle. She didn't move nearly as fast as him, thankfully, and when I caught her I could feel that she wasn't as strong, either. I yanked her into the air, dragging him along by his teeth, buried so unhelpfully in my upper thigh. I could tell he was going for the artery, so once we got aloft I sparked off Gavrikov, setting fire to my leg. He yelped, and I grabbed him by the scruff of the neck as he cut loose and started to drop, carrying him along into the night.

"Wh-where are you taking us?" the woman asked. She didn't sound scared, which just annoyed me more. I looked down and saw my reflection, complete with my odd cargo. Does carrying these two stooges make me look fat? I wondered as I watched his grey hair and his bathrobe flap in the wind. I looked up again and ignored that reflection, because it was giving me a view I really didn't care for.

I didn't answer her inquiry, because I hadn't fully decided yet. I just tightened my grip on her leg and the back of his neck, making sure I didn't lose my prizes, and flew off into the western sky.

10.

Ma

"We've got a … minor problem here," Cassidy said, dripping on the floor. She'd popped out of the tank without bothering to dry off first, and now she was just standing there in the kitchen, dripping all over the place. Ma kept her peace about it, though, because there wasn't anything to be done about it now. She'd already left a trail clear back to the corner of the living room, surely, since she couldn't exactly fly.

"What is it, sweet cheeks?" Ma asked, putting on her best smile. She'd had about enough of these particular houseguests, especially since they'd long ago overstayed their welcome. She looked sidelong at Denise, who was standing with her back to the oven, arms folded over her husky frame, more than a little disgusted at the sight of field mouse Cassidy drenched from head to toe and barely stuffed in that skimpy wetsuit-looking thing.

"Sienna got to the assassins I hired," Cassidy sniffled. Ma couldn't imagine that water being too good for anyone, not long term. "She burned down their house, captured them—"

"What do they know?" Ma jumped right ahead to the pertinent point. She had rolls in the oven and they were coming up on done.

"Nothing, really," Cassidy said and hugged herself tight, lips a little blue now that she was out of that warm salt water.

37

Ma had the windows open, because it was a perfect autumn day for it. "I hired them over the net, so—"

"Well, if they don't know anything," Ma said, making her way over to the oven, brushing Denise aside and prompting a scowl—that girl had no gratitude, even when she'd be grabbing a roll and buttering it in two minutes—never took her eyes off Cassidy the whole time, "I wouldn't worry about it. Can't tell her what they don't know."

"I didn't think she'd be able to find them," Cassidy said, sullen. She got like that when things didn't go her way, like she couldn't imagine being outsmarted. Ma could imagine it easily, because she kept seeing it happen. Simmons had done it quite a lot, even down to this last trip he'd taken without her. Sure, he'd said he was going with Denise and Junior, but she knew he didn't, and they knew he didn't. He wasn't stupid, he gave an excuse why they should believe him, why he needed to get away, but she had a good enough read on him to know he was stepping out on the shivering waif that was dripping on her linoleum.

"Well, these things happen," Ma said, feeling the blast of the oven opening up right in her face. She shifted her skin to vulcanized rubber as she grabbed the metal pan out with a bare, black hand. Didn't hurt a bit. She pulled the rolls out and set them on top of the electric coils on the stovetop, letting the metals meet with a rattle as the baking pan found its balance. She shifted back to human skin and snatched a towel from behind Denise, prompting another petulant scowl, and crossed over to Cassidy, stooping down to mop up some of the dripping the girl was doing. "Why don't you go make sure that you've covered your tracks up good?"

Cassidy made a face at her grammar, couldn't even hide it. The girl was snooty, and that got under Ma's skin more than a little. She'd tolerated it up until now, because of the promise of a painful death for Sienna Nealon. Oh, she'd talked a good game, Cassidy had, but she was all hat and no cattle. Plan after plan, and every one of them had fallen short because Cassidy couldn't account for human behavior, not being much of a human herself.

Ma waited until she heard the tell-tale click of the sensory deprivation tank shutting before she let out a sigh of relief. "Denise," she snapped, "get the wet-dry vac in here and clean up that carpet."

"I don't want to do it," Denise said, like Ma'd just asked her to pick up a piece of poo bare-handed.

"Well, I don't want it mildewing in here," Ma said. "It's gonna smell worse than that week we went down to Odessa and Junior let the dogs stay in." The boy hadn't even bothered to get up in the middle of the night and let 'em out. Twelve dogs, no relief, and when she got back she came within an inch of skinning that boy alive.

"Unnnnnh," Denise said, sounding like a sixteen year old, which she'd left behind almost a decade ago. Ingrate. But she hauled herself off in the direction of the storage closet to get the vacuum.

Ma mopped up a little bit more of the water, as best she could, until the towel was saturated. She lifted it up and stared at it, watched the water drip down her fingers. She felt a lot like the towel; it'd had about all the water it could, and she'd had about enough Cassidy to last her a lifetime. If the girl had been able to deliver on even one of her promises, Ma might have felt differently. But instead she'd dragged Anselmo and Simmons out of prison to no use at all. Anselmo was dead; Sienna Nealon was alive. Ma stared at the tank in the corner of the living room and let her mind drift, thinking for the thousandth time how she was going to take care of this particular problem once this thing was all over with.

And she knew, for sure, it wasn't going to end up messy like Cassidy's plans. It was going to end up messy of the sort she'd need a wet-dry vac and maybe a steamer to clean up.

11.

Sienna

I marched my two prisoners into the detention block in headquarters without much in the way of mercy for slacking off. The woman, whose name was Rosanna Borosky, had offered a little resistance when we landed. I'd punched her in the kidney and she'd stopped, but not before I got a hint of her meta strength. It wasn't anything special; that much was clear. Low-scale stuff, whatever she was.

No, iron tooth Michael Shafer was my main problem, and he wasn't presenting much of one at the moment. He was still looking a little woozy from my "interrogation" of him. She was a lot more functional at this point, actually, but she knew about as much as he did. They'd taken the contract via the internet, and a little more hastily than they normally would have, apparently, because they'd been recommended by a trusted third party to this particular client. That was why most of the instructions had been out in the open rather than over an encrypted chat app of the sort the Brain had favored in the past.

She'd put a hit out on me and/or Reed—this wasn't clear, because she'd just told them to wire his car—only an hour or two before it had actually blown up. So, not long before Anselmo and his protégé had tangled with Reed for the last time, Cassidy had ordered a special delivery of death to our campus. It was a move that would have reeked of desperation had it been a normal bomb, but the Brain hadn't wanted a normal bomb. Oh, no, she asked for the deluxe, enough to kill a normal human five times over, even if they pulled a Robert De Niro in *Casino* and put a metal plate under their entire car.

I strolled the two of them, entirely dazed and with all the spine busted right out of them (not literally—I know you leap right to that because it's me, but not this time) right up to the door to the prison without bothering to cuff them.

I didn't need to cuff them. I'd just used my powers to steal the memories I needed right out of their heads. Normally I might not have, but these were special circumstances, and if I'd had to interrogate them without my succubus powers, I wouldn't have bothered even asking civilized questions. I would have probably escalated straight to alternating between dunking them upside down into Lake Minnetonka and setting them on fire. Know thy enemy, know thyself, and thyself was not in a mood that encouraged trifling.

"Two to go down," I said to the guard, Rogers, who regarded me with a carefully neutral look and my prisoners with one that indicated that they were contaminated with toxic waste in his eyes.

"Uhhh ..." Rogers said, clutching tighter to his M4 assault rifle. He pointed the barrel down and far, far away from me, then mumbled his next words. "I can't let you down there."

"The hell you say?" I asked.

"Can't let you down there," Rogers said, slightly less tentatively. Maybe his boys dropped.

"I've got prisoners," I clarified for him without smacking him over the head or anything. Go thyself.

"You're, uh ... suspended," he said, and like a mouse he whispered the last part, bringing a hand off the grip and scratching a sudden itch on his face.

"You know that big-ass explosion on campus a couple hours ago?" I fixed him in my gaze and he didn't dare look up. He looked like he was feeling itchy. Must have been nerves. "These are the responsible parties. They are also metas. What the hell would you have me do with them if not put them in our meta prison? Because … maybe I'll just drop them at your house."

"It's orders, Ms. Nealon," Rogers said, looking especially pained at the mention of his house. "From the top. You're suspended, you can't arrest anybody, per the orders of the—"

"Director," I muttered in the same tone as Jerry Seinfeld would say, "Newman." "Is he in this morning?"

Rogers looked like he wanted to pace, possibly leaving his skin behind. His hand was back on the M4's grip, and he was white-knuckling it. "I … I don't know."

"Okay, then," I said, and turned loose of the two of them, both nearly collapsing, looking around with slack looks as they felt my grip release. "I'll just leave them here for you, then."

"Uhhh …" Rogers's eyes went wide, he looked a little panicked. He was at the outside duty station, wasn't even at the inner door to the prison. He just kept an eye on the lobby entrance with an assault rifle, was the first line of defense. "You—you can't do that!"

"They're prisoners without a prison to go to," I said, and started to walk away.

"W-wait!" Rogers called. "Don't leave them here!"

"You think the Director wants me to take them to his office?" I asked, walking away a lot slower than I could have, all for effect. Rogers looked a couple steps shy of panic, the end of his M4 wavering as he pondered bringing it up against Shafer and Borosky, who, while still not having their wits entirely about them, were clearly starting to steer their slow wits to the idea that they might be able to make a break for it. "He gets mad when I don't take my winter boots off before I come visit. Doubt he's going to respond well to me bringing assassins in."

"You can't just leave them here!" Rogers called, trotting that old chestnut again.

"Well, gosh, Rogers," I said, realizing that I didn't even know his first name. "I can't take them with me, so ..." I shrugged, as though helpless. Borosky stood up straight, and I figured Rogers had about three seconds to make a decision that was probably a lot more difficult than his usual fare. Beef or chicken, Rogers? Bud or Michelob? Death or dishonor?

"Okayokayokay!" he shouted, waving a hand in surrender while clutching tight to the M4 with the other, barrel only a few degrees off from pointing at Borosky's head. Those few degrees would matter in about a second, but fortunately for him, I was quicker.

I swept Borosky and Shafer off their feet, crossing the distance between us and slamming their faces into the tile floor. Excessive force? Nonsense. These people were killers, and given half a chance they'd rip Rogers to pieces and take his M4 as a prize for their wall—if I hadn't burnt all of them down.

I put a knee on each of their backs and then put their shirts between my hand and the back of their necks, enough to give me some nice grip on their scruff but enough cloth between us that I wouldn't drain their souls.

"Oh hell," Rogers muttered, blinking at the speed with which I'd done my thing. "Oh hell, what am I doing?"

"Your job," I said, hauling the prisoners to their feet as Rogers opened the door behind him with a key card, looking nervous as a cat in a room full of dogs, sweat pouring down his temples. "Funny that I have to remind you of what it really is, since I'm the one on suspension." And I frogmarched them both down into the prison, knowing full well that my next argument was going to be with a man who wouldn't respond with nearly as much flop-sweat to my bluffs.

12.

"You just deposited two prisoners downstairs while on suspension," Andrew Phillips said as I opened the door to his office and strolled in uninvited. He was sitting behind his desk, the sun not quite up yet, the glow of his computer monitor lighting his face with pale color. He didn't deign to look at me, and whether it was because he thought I wouldn't hurt him or because he somehow thought himself immune to harm, I didn't know. "What are you doing?"

I also didn't care. "I'm on a mission from God," I said in my best Midwestern accent. "And if you know I dropped those two down there, I assume you also know why I did it?"

"J.J. forwarded me the pertinent intel." Phillips looked up, impassive as ever, his large head perched atop broad shoulders. He was a big guy. And the bigger they are, the harder I tend to hit them, because that generally meant they were more of a threat. "What happened when you showed up?"

"They threw explosive chemicals in my face and tried to blow my head off," I said. "Best first date I've had in months."

He processed that, his eyes not moving. "What do you want me to do with them?"

"Your job," I spat back acidly. "I just policed a metahuman threat and responded to it. Don't block me now."

"You're the one who's suspended," he said, like I needed another reminder. "It's *not* your job right now. Besides, you're on a mission from God." He didn't add the Dan Aykroyd accent when he said it. "Not from the U.S. government."

"Can you even tell the difference between the two on any given day?" Maybe this wasn't the time to mouth off, I hear you saying. I hear you now; but then I was without any reason to think mouthing off as anything other than my best option.

"One's wrathful," he said, in the closest I'd ever heard to a quip from him, "and one's just incompetent."

"Where do you stand in all this, Phillips?" I asked, fixing him with a hard gaze. I suspected his knees were not exactly knocking under the desk.

"You're suspended," he said, repeating his mantra again. I wonder if he said it during morning meditation. "You don't work here right now. You're a private citizen, and you can't go around arresting people, especially not on a personal vendetta. Which is not a mission from God *or* the federal government."

"Which one is incompetent, again?" I pursed my lips real thin. "Whoever this Brain is, she's an eminent threat."

"To you."

"She blew up a car in the middle of a government installation tonight," I snapped. "Conspired to poison a federal agent in a scheme that almost resulted in something on the order of a nuclear bomb going off on the fringe of a major metropolitan area, and you, as head of this agency, don't seem to give a damn. I think I figured out which one is incompetent, and I just wish I could see a little wrath—"

"You were the one who almost blew up the metro," Phillips said coolly, and got to his feet, buttoning his suit jacket. "If you go off looking for this Brain while you're still pissed off, what's the likelihood you stay calm enough not to get civilians hurt or killed in the process?"

"You think I'm flying off all furiously angry?" I asked.

"Wrathful," he said. "Fits better. You've been where you're standing before." He folded his arms. "Do I need to say it?"

"Say what?" I got out through lips that were so tight with anger they didn't want to move.

"Parks, Clary, Kappler, Bastian." He was an implacable monument carved out of the middle of the office. "Wrath."

It was like having someone hold up a mirror to show you the giant mud pie dripping down your face. "I've got two assassins in the prison below that say differently. Still breathing. Wrath reserved."

"What happens to the ones who really did it?" he asked, watching for my response. "Not just the weapon used, what happens to the finger that pulled the trigger?" He stared at me hard, like he really wanted to know. "Are you gonna reserve it then, too? Or am I going to have another PR mess of biblical proportions to clean up?"

I held back from answering immediately with the cheap snark. I held back the good snark, too, in hopes that age would make it better. It was a battle just to control my emotions, not to throw an easy witticism at him, something appropriate for me but not for anyone who had a brain or an appreciation for civil conversation. "I—"

His phone beeped and he didn't even hesitate to interrupt our conversation. "Go." He put it on speakerphone, even. What a dick.

"Sir," came the clear tone of his assistant, whom I hadn't even seen when I came in, "NASA has sent us a FLASH emergency brief—"

"What is it?" Phillips asked.

His assistant skipped a couple lines, undeterred. "There's a meteor the size of a Metrolink bus on course for Lake Michigan at the moment, due for splashdown in about twenty minutes. It's projected to impact twenty miles off Chicago."

Phillips blinked, still calm as all hell. "And?"

His assistant paused, leaving hissing dead air. "They're wondering if we can do anything about it."

Phillips gave me that dead-eyed stare. "Can we do anything about that?"

I seethed inside, months of bitterness writhing like a fiery snake in my belly, waiting to come out with a hiss and a pop of flame. "We? Probably not? Me? Maybe, but I'm suspended." I threw that out there, just wanting to see what he'd say.

"Yes, you are," he said with a light shrug, and at that moment I realized that if the end of the world was stampeding toward us right now, he'd still be citing regulation and procedure to the moment of impact. "But what are you going to do about it?"

I wanted to burn him to death right there and leave a charred, blackened corpse behind, but I didn't. I just looked at him with enough fury that if I had said Gavrikov's name in my head right then, spontaneous combustion would have occurred.

Kill him, Wolfe whispered, not for the first time in the last few weeks.

You should totally do that, Kappler agreed.

It would be so satisfying, Bjorn added.

"Shut up," I whispered, and Phillips's eyebrows drew up in slight surprise. I stared at him, seething.

"Sir?" his assistant's voice came again. "Nineteen minutes to impact, and NASA is wondering if we can help." Phillips stared at me, I stared at Phillips, and it was a game of chicken for the ages. "Sir?" his assistant's voice came again.

I blinked first. I summoned up Wolfe's power as I blew out the window, contenting myself with going to supersonic speeds about six feet away from him, knowing the shockwave would probably knock him flat on his ass as I hauled my own to Chicago at top speed.

13.

Timing is everything, they say, and by "they," I mean some jackass who never had to stop a meteor from destroying Chicago while they were trying to chase down the person who blew up their brother. Here in the real world, though, that was exactly what I had to do, and I did it in the manner of my generation, griping mentally about my ordeal the entire time.

"I can't just kill Andrew Phillips," I said, not even close to audible as the force of air rushing past my face mushed my cheeks like the sweet and plump aunt I'd never had. Mine was a psycho, full stop, and any pinching of cheeks on her part would probably have been the kind that would break skin.

Could, Wolfe said, saying the same shit he'd been spouting for weeks now. *Should.*

It would not be difficult, Bjorn said. *You have done it to others for less.*

"What?" I almost dropped out of the sky from outrage at that one. How dare the crazed Nordic psycho impugn my reputation. "No, I haven't!"

Rick, Zack said tentatively. He wasn't on their side by any means and had regularly proven himself the not-devil's advocate in these ceaseless debates that the six numb-no-skulls in my head were having constantly nowadays. The Primus of Omega.

"That was different," I snapped, the wind pressure on my cheeks probably resulting in it sounding like "wah wah wiffwent!" Whatever. They were in my head, they knew what I was saying. I wouldn't even have been talking out loud, but such was the measure of the "had enough of this shit" lines in the graduated cylinder of my patience that it was simply overflowing at this point.

Friendly fire, Roberto Bastian suggested. *Sometimes a butterbars gets out of line, is going to get the squad killed—*

"Naw hewah!" I said, meaning, "Not helping!"

Far be it from me to suggest anything that would actually benefit you, Eve Kappler said, *but this man is a disaster for the agency.*

A disaster in addition to constantly stepping all over your former girlfriend, you mean to say, I said, silently this time.

I could almost see Kappler's cheeks flush in my head. *Fine. You figured me out. But he's far more of a pain in your ass and a credible threat to you than that Russian woman you dropped out of the sky a few months ago.*

I couldn't argue with that, so I didn't. *I cannot. Kill. The head. Of my agency.* When did I become the voice of reason and tolerance and kindasorta nonviolence?

Then again, compared to some of these people in my head, I was almost like Gandhi.

It would almost certainly lead back to you, Aleksandr Gavrikov agreed. *Gone are the days when she had unlimited discretion to mop up these problems—*

The hell, Gavrikov? I thought at him.

It's true, he said with what would have been a shrug, if he hadn't been disembodied. *The time was that the curtains were pulled, when a metahuman could conduct their life as they were meant to, free from oversight and criticism over every little thing.* I could feel Bjorn and Wolfe nodding along with him. Well, not nodding, but … whatever, agreeing. *We were gods. Now you are people, and subject to the laws of man.*

I am no man, I said, clearly channeling the spirit of Miranda Otto.

You're not exactly a Shieldmaiden of Rohan, either, though, Zack offered helpfully, getting my reference immediately. He should have; he was the one who introduced me to the *Lord of the Rings* movies. *And Gav's got a point.* How many years exactly into their forced incarceration in my brain had my ex started calling nutball flame-warrior Aleksandr Gavrikov "Gav"? *There's watchful eyes aplenty, now. She can't just assert her will, go after these people like she would have before—*

I didn't know if I should feel insulted by the implication that I was some sort of hanging-on-the-edge-by-my-fingernails psychotic waiting to snap before, but it bothered me a little. It was a thread that had run through my life since the day Zack had died, a piece of my past. I'd killed people, and I'd not really been that shy about it in some cases. Part of me even questioned where the line was at this point, whether I'd moved it over time. I knew which dead bodies I felt guilty about and which ones I didn't, though, and the ones I felt guilty about were the ones farthest back in the past, the ones where I'd responded to Wolfe's suggestion more strongly than I should have, or maybe just let him push me slightly in the direction he wanted me to go.

—all I'm saying is that she's changed, Zack said

Hunters never change, Wolfe said. *Always seeking their prey.*

Revenge doesn't exactly go out of style, Kappler added. *When someone challenges you as she's been challenged, to show weakness is to invite further challenge.*

She's the apex predator on this planet, Bjorn said. *Without fear, she's simply the largest target—*

—trouble could come knocking any time, Bastian said, *and now they're actively interfering with her doing her duty—*

This, ladies and gentlemen, is why I took a shot of chloridamide a few days ago that nearly killed a lot of people. It had been like this since even before the suspension, a constant argument over direction. I raised my eyes to look at the horizon and they burned at the wind blasting my lids back. The human body wasn't really meant to fly this fast without a plane around it. There were g-forces I had to account for, I had to be careful of how I positioned my neck (I'd broken it one time by accelerating too fast without Wolfe's power at my immediate disposal—that had almost resulted in death), I had to not look straight into the wind for too long, I had to maintain a lower altitude, to keep Wolfe front and center the whole time so as to keep my circulatory system from—

It was a lot to remember. As I looked into the sunrise and saw a trail of fire coming down at an angle from the sky, I realized that this was maybe not going to be the easiest job I'd ever done.

"I need to think while I'm doing this," I said, speaking aloud to make sure everyone knew I was serious. The argument quieted, blissfully, though only for now, I was sure. I pulled everyone to the front of my mind, making sure there was agreement, and then I zoomed at the chunk of falling rock that was heading down fast, passing the gleaming towers of Chicago as I went to save the city from a tsunami that they didn't even know was coming.

14.

Being somewhat pressed for time, I had to come up with a strategy to stop a giant segment of flaming, falling rock on the fly. While this may sound to an idiot as simple as, I dunno, getting underneath it and catching it, I was (probably) not an idiot and saw a few issues with that strategy.

Giant hunk of rock that's hotter than hell courtesy of the resistance of the atmosphere to its extremely fast descent hits one hundred and ... uh ... something ... pound girl who's either floating still or flying toward it. I didn't know the specific velocity of the meteor and it didn't matter for my purposes, because I could figure out how it was going to end—either in me going SPLAT or it breaking into smaller pieces and wreaking some other form of havoc as its component parts spun off course. I tried to imagine how the press would react to a Buick-sized piece of meteor I smashed hitting the John Hancock tower. "Hey, but I saved the city from a flood!" I would protest.

SIENNA NEALON MURDERS A THOUSAND INNOCENT CHICAGOANS AND PROBABLY AT LEAST SIX DOZEN PUPPIES WHILE ENCOURAGING TEENAGE SMOKING, is how the headline would read. Buzzfeed would add me to their *Which historical mass murderer are you?* quiz.

The SPLAT might be better.

I suspected I might maybe be able to survive the impact if

I ran into it. I had survived contact with a plane before, with jumping out of a plane before, with—well, hell, a lot of impacts that shouldn't have been possible. But none of those objects had been flaming from entry into a resistant atmosphere, which brought me to problem two—how hot was this thing burning, anyway?

Being neither a physicist nor a math-magician, these were also questions I could not answer.

All I had was a layman's knowledge of the problem at hand and an expert's knowledge of all the different ways the press would try to screw me if I messed up even slightly. Now that NASA had asked for help and, presumably, Phillips had let them know I was on the case, I had successfully worked my way into a damned if you do, shagged rectally with a pointy object if you don't position. I did not enjoy it, but this was my life of late. Couldn't stand up for falling down, couldn't succeed for being pushed down to failure, and couldn't make a good impression for all these people trying to make me a pariah.

I tried not to wonder how many of these assholes were actually in Chicago as I streaked toward the incoming meteor. I thought about the innocent people who were just going about their day on the shores of Lake Michigan, looking up into the sky as they—I dunno, walked their children and dogs and pet ferrets while discussing all the charity work they were going to do today.

I flew over Lake Michigan lower than I probably needed to, making a wake in the water behind me. It was kind of soothing, and I decided that I should be allowed to indulge myself a little before I went to confront a flaming meteor. Meteorite? Hell if I knew. FIERY DEATH. That's what it was.

I swallowed and looked skyward, and once I found it, I shot into the air on an intercept course. I estimated I had about two minutes to impact, which, hey, was not a ton of time to figure out how to do something I'd never actually done before. "Invulnerable skin would have been real useful right now," I muttered as I felt the sting of the air in my eyes and across my flesh. There was no looking down now. "Superman's got it easy."

There was a reluctant chorus of agreement in my head. I could tell they all wanted to resume their fight. It was like walking into a party where nobody was speaking. You just feel the tension in the air. I shot into the sky toward the falling star, fully aware that there was no camera watching me now, not at this distance from the actual city. Time to be an unsung hero—again.

I shot wide past the meteor, giving it enough berth that I didn't get caught in its wash, letting it blow past as I used Gavrikov to absorb some heat as it streaked by. I'd already flipped and was chasing it by the time it got a hundred feet past me, and was doing my level best to match speed as it streaked toward the lake below. It was a hell of a lot bigger than a metro bus, closer probably in size to two Abrahms tanks welded to each other.

I pulled heat as fast as I could, absorbing the meteor's contrail as I caught up and flew past the leading edge of the damned thing. It was fairly oblong and I overshot it by a few feet per second and then slowed, my hands extended to "catch" it as best I could catch a multi-ton object streaking through the atmosphere. I looked down and saw nothing but water coming up fast.

"This is what heroes do," I muttered to myself like there was some sort of consolation in those words as I started to apply the brakes, the torsional forces working across my entire body, tensing me enough that I felt like I was about to have a full-body stroke. My palms and arms got the worst of it, if there was such a thing as the worst of it, and I was forced to unlock my elbows in order to take some of the tension off of them. I kept the meteor from crashing right into my neck and killing me, but it still thumped me good when it ended up on my shoulders.

I had it like Atlas had the world, the weight of it slowly being taken up as I started to gradually turn gravity on again. I was taking the heat in across the entire surface of my body, burning up the third set of clothing I'd wasted today. Yeah. It was one of those kind of days. Barely dawn and I was about to end up naked again. It happens so often lately I don't even mention it anymore, like when I got burned out of my clothes at Shafer's house. Yeah. That fight was near naked. I'd left Shafer and Borosky on my balcony while they were still disoriented from the mind meld and put on clothes in speedy rush.

Anyway, at least there was some upside to not having cameras around.

I took up more of the meteor's weight as it pushed me toward the lake below. I judged it to be less than five thousand feet below, but my perspective was kind of iffy since I was presently on the leading edge of a catastrophic event fast approaching a major U.S. city.

I pushed against the meteor and it pushed against me with gravity and momentum on its side. It hurt a lot, not gonna lie. I pushed back even harder, and felt something near my kidney explode. Tendons blew out in my neck. One of my arms shattered, and it cascaded down into my shoulder and snapped my collarbone.

My Wolfe powers held me together. Barely. You can always tell it's getting bad when Wolfe starts to panic. *Little Doll* ...

"I got it," I breathed, but in truth, I wasn't sure I did. My body was trying to pull itself together, but it wasn't exactly doing a bang-up job under the pressure.

You might have reached your limit on this one, Sienna, Zack said.

Let it go! Kappler advised, more emotional than I'd ever heard her. *Get out while you can!*

"No," I grunted as we slipped to within a thousand feet of Lake Michigan below. I fired a few rounds of Eve's light nets into the meteor, doubtful they'd do any good but also fairly sure they wouldn't do any harm. I didn't feel any difference, but then I had a few tons resting on my neck by now, and I hadn't even taken up the full weight of the thing just yet.

This is suicide, Bjorn said, probably taking in my view of the lake and realizing that, yep, we were about to hit that, and still going awfully fast. Not a survival speed for a human, even absent the massive rock that was coming along for the ride.

"At least I brought something to mark my watery grave," I said. I looked sidelong and saw the city of Chicago off to my left, in the far distance, towers sticking up into the sky, sunrise reflected shining orange against some of the buildings. It was like a beacon against the horizon. Children. Puppies. Charity workers.

All counting on me.

I arrested my downward momentum, taking up the full weight of the meteor on my shoulders, and boy, did I feel it. It broke my back, both shoulders, a dozen ribs (on each side), and it was my only good fortune was that I managed to heal them all before they became much more than fractures. My muscles strained, squealed, cried—actually, that might just have been me. There were tears of pure pain running down my face as my feet touched the water and halted with it around my ankles.

I stood there, a couple inches from walking on water with a few tons of weight on my shoulders and let my eyes dart about. I took a ragged breath, then another. The surface of Lake Michigan stretched for miles in every direction, and a cool breeze blew over my bare skin, which hurt just about everywhere. "Well, hell," I said, and realized that the surface of the rock that was eating into my back was as cool as if it had just been plucked off the ground, "what do I do with this now?"

15.

I was body conscious enough to make the flight back to Minneapolis with my skin on fire, having left the meteor on the bottom of Lake Michigan after easing it in so as to avoid any massive tidal waves. It wasn't like I could just carry the damned thing off, after all, so I did the best I could with it. It's not like I wanted it for a souvenir or something, a fine reminder of that time I saved Chicago. Nobody would believe me anyhow, and the press would probably report that I ripped the top off Everest or something just to show off.

By the time I'd slipped into my fourth change of clothes for the day that was now dawning properly, the knock sounded at my door that heralded another impending discussion that I probably didn't want to have.

Of course, the knock hadn't actually come at my door; it had come on the drywall just inside my door because I didn't currently have a door. "Uh, come in," I said, resigning myself to the likelihood that I was about to get a lecture from some quarter.

Quinton Zollers strolled into my apartment as though he didn't have to just navigate over my kicked-in door, as though the place didn't still stink to high heaven like someone had used it for a latrine. Which ... they sort of had. He had his hands clasped behind his back, and he looked around like he hadn't been in here just a few hours earlier and already seen the place in its current state of disrepair. "So ..."

"That's a lousy opener for someone who can read my mind," I said as I put on my leather jacket. It wasn't my favorite, because there was no way I was risking wearing something I actually liked on a day like today.

"Just because I can read your mind doesn't mean I always know what to say." His eyes ran over my kitchen. "Because sometimes you don't even know what you want to hear."

"You know what I *don't* want to hear right now." The jacket settled on my shoulders, more comfortable than the giant slab of space rock that had been on them only a few minutes earlier. "That's a starting point, right?"

"You're not in the mood for a challenge, I know." He took a few more steps into the room and cocked his head at my dog, sleeping on the heating grate in the living room. "But, then, who enjoys being challenged?"

"I've got enough of those coming my way on any given day, let alone today," I said, holstering a spare gun. I hadn't even carried one earlier, when I'd done my various vengeful runnings around this morning. "But you're right, I don't like arguing with the people I know. Feels a little too much like what I get from every other quarter."

"'Our critics are our friends, they show us our faults,'" he said, looking at me with a reserved amusement that would have made me want to kill anyone else I saw wearing the expression.

"Then I've got a shit-ton of friends."

"No, you actually don't, by any other standard," he said, jabbing me for the first time in a long damned time.

"Thanks for the reminder," I sniped back.

"At this point, a lot of people consider you invulnerable, power-wise," he said as I started past him. "Yet you're one of the most wounded people I've ever met."

I stopped, showing him nothing but my back. "I wasn't always invulnerable, and you know it."

"And now you never let yourself be vulnerable in any way."

"The last time I did," I said, turning around to look at him with one of those dangerous looks I usually reserved for others, "you know what happened."

"You trusted, Winter betrayed you," he said, "I get that. You've got history."

"Yeah," I said, smirking because I didn't want to let him see how I was really feeling. Not that I could hide it from him, but still, I didn't want to feel exposed. That's why I put on clothes, after all. "You know I didn't quite grow up in the cupboard under the stairs on Privet Drive, but ..." I paused, thinking about it. "Actually, maybe I had it worse."

"You keep talking about your history," Zollers said, "but I'm here to talk about your destiny."

"My destiny at the moment involves finding more people to hammer into the ground," I said, adjusting the leather coat around my shoulders. It felt damned uncomfortable after flying with flaming skin for a while.

"You begged me to stay here," Zollers said, bringing me up short. "Why?"

"You know why," I said, and I could tell my face was ashen.

"I am rather calloused to pain," he said, and he took a couple steps toward me, looking at his feet all the while. "I have walls. Defenses. It's a natural thing to develop when the thoughts of others start breaking into your own in your teenage years, when you don't even know who you are yet. The struggles of others ... now, that's pain. Pain funneled right into the center of you. A six-lane freeway of raw, bare nerves."

"Yes, I'm familiar with pain," I said.

"Of course you are," he said. "You've been feeling it on a near-constant basis since before then. Not that of others, though, just your own significant amounts of it."

"I know you're coming to a point here."

"Why?" he asked, and now it was his turn to smirk slightly. "Do you have somewhere else to be, or do you just want to wander around beating up random strangers as you try to get a line on what to do next?" That took a little bit of my defiance away, and I knew he sensed it. "I feel your pain like no other, is my point. I get it. It's unique on a level that I don't experience much, but it's also the same as that of everyone else."

"So, what are you aiming for here?" I asked. "You want me to talk about it? How I feel after seeing my brother in the hospital, tubes coming out of him because of people who hate me? How I reacted to his girlfriend telling me she doesn't blame me, when—I mean, hell, she damned well should." I took a breath, and it felt hot in my skin. "You know how I feel about all of this, all of it, and—"

"I don't, actually," he said, staring me down. "Because sometimes, especially at a moment like this … you don't know how you feel, either."

"I know how I—" I paused right in the middle of my sentence, and tried to take inventory. I knew rage. Blinding, angry, yeah, that was there.

"That's level one," he agreed. "Like the icing on the cake, it's something we can all see."

"I'm sure the gooey center beneath has some more of the sugary same," I quipped, not feeling that witty.

"You're reacting," he said. "You don't know exactly what you're going to do, you're just flying like a missile, going after whatever heat source crosses your path. That's dangerous, especially for you—"

"Because I've killed before?" I smiled bitterly.

"Because you're the most powerful woman in the world," he said, serious.

"Because I'm dangerous," I said.

"You're capable of it," he agreed, though I could sense it was only partially. "But you're also capable of good, like any other person. I think you should have seen that plainly after this morning."

"This morning I burned down a house and dragged its

occupants kicking and screaming to prison," I said, and my shoulders slumped, "and I drained their memories looking for any hint that they knew who hired them to do ... this thing."

"To kill you," he said. I looked at him and my mouth fell open a little hearing him verbalize it. "That's the thing they were doing. They may have bombed your brother's car, and that may be what makes you angry about it all, but ... they tried to kill you, Sienna. The Brain is trying to kill you."

"Who hasn't tried that before?" I asked, weariness settling in on me as I recovered my composure.

"At some point you're going to have to reconcile your feelings about that," he said, "because—"

My phone chirped at me, and like Phillips before me, I was the asshole that answered it trying to find a way out of this uncomfortable conversation. Zollers's face registered a note of surprise that he concealed expertly before I spoke. "Hello?"

"Hey," J.J. said, a little tentative. "I have something for you."

"Let it be a face to punch."

"Uhh ... not mine, I hope?" J.J. asked, sounding a little worried.

"I don't punch your face," I said, "I just hover over it ominously until you wake up screaming while looking into my angry, sensual eyes."

"Uhhh ..."

"J.J.," I said, dropping the smartassery. "What?"

"Those emails," J.J. said, "I'm not done sorting yet, but I got a fresh contact on something that just came through. A bartender as near as I can tell, someone who's doing some ongoing work for your Brain—"

"The Brain employs its own bartenders?" I paused, eyes flitting around as I processed that. "It must have a hell of a drinking problem—"

"—and he's got, like, spy reports," J.J. went on,

apparently knowing when to ignore me, "about you."

I paused, letting that sink in. "Spy reports?"

"Yeah," J.J. said. "Like, real intelligence gathering stuff. I searched back through the history of emails from this guy, and this bartender has been sending some real nasty nuggets to the Brain, stuff she's been sending to reporters everywhere—"

I saw red, and I knew by the look on Zollers's face that he knew that crimson was my color today. "Oh, my," he said.

"Hey," came a voice from outside the door. "Anyone in here?" Augustus Coleman peeked around the corner and looked straight at me, then Zollers. "Sorry. You left your door, uh … on the floor."

I looked down at my hand, which shook, and I knew in that moment that the frosty cake of my emotions was definitely hiding veins of anger throughout, like chocolate. Sweet, vengeful chocolate. "Name and address," I said, and my phone beeped before I even finished saying it, the map popping up automatically.

"Way ahead of y—" J.J. said as I hung up.

"Sienna—" Zollers started to say.

"Don't." I breathed in through my nose, out through my mouth. I came up with a solution before I'd even had time to think it through. "If you're that worried, you can come with me."

"Is this a field trip?" Augustus asked, his head sticking out from behind the scuffed wall. He looked better without the cervical collar. "Because I *need* to get out of here for a little while. Think those pain meds made me all itchy inside."

"Sure," I said, stalking my way around the corner and out the door. I could sense Dr. Zollers following me, and Augustus behind him, could hear their footsteps even as they tried to be quiet enough not to waken the furious crazy that was leading the procession. "The more the merrier." Even though I knew that when I found this bartender, there damned sure wasn't going to be much merriness to be had for anyone but the funeral parlor that got to bill for overtime after scraping him back together.

16.

I broke down the door without regard for property, or a warrant, or public safety, or … well, much of anything, really. It busted inward, swung on a shattered frame, and hung in my way until I just ripped it off with a second hit and sent it spiraling into the drywall behind it.

"Honey, I'm home," I said as I pushed my way inside and saw someone spring up off a couch to my left, coughing on a cigarette that dangled between astonished lips and that flew out on the next good hacking. It gave the room a stink, that lit cigarette, reminding me a little of when I'd breathed in the toxic burning of a car's interior a few hours earlier.

The smoker in question was a shade under six feet, skinny, heavily tattooed, wearing nothing but boxer shorts and clearly scared shitless by the sight of someone crashing into his house without announcement. I knew from what J.J. had sent me that this bartender's name was Charles O'Shea. He didn't look Irish to me, though sometimes it's tough to tell when someone's scared shitless.

He bolted for the archway behind him, where I could see a dining room, and I caught up with him before he got more than a few steps, seizing hold of his naked shoulders and shoving him roughly into the waiting arms of Augustus, who had followed behind me. He grabbed the guy with a little nervous gusto, like he was afraid he was going to get caught doing something he shouldn't have.

I walked over and stubbed out the cigarette with my boot on the carpet, but I doubted it was going to cost him a security deposit since by the look of the place he'd lost that a long time ago. There were holes in the walls, probably a hundred dollars' worth of stereo equipment that looked like it had been dragged right out of the seventies surrounding one of those old-school widescreen TVs, the sort that weighs tons because it has to project the image on the front of the TV like a movie theater exists inside the huge contraption. "The hell?" I wondered, looking at it all. "Is this some kind of mania for vintage or do you just not have the money for a modern flatscreen?"

"Picture's better on this," he asserted, surprisingly defiant for a guy who was being held in something close to a submission hold whilst nearly naked by a pretty tall man, while a humorless woman picked over his choice in electronics.

"Yeah," Augustus said, "and eight tracks sound better than CDs."

I eased closer to the guy and caught sight of the fear in his eyes. "You know who I am?"

He blinked, looking left and catching sight of Zollers. "No," he said sullenly.

I didn't even need to look at Zollers to know he was lying. "That was a rhetorical question," I said. "Everyone knows who I am."

"Try to pretend like you don't enjoy it," he scoffed, with way more courage than I would have had in his utter-lack-of-shoes.

"Hey, I know this guy," Augustus said, turning Charles's head to look at his face in profile. "This is your brother's bartender."

Augustus was an honest man, and while that wasn't a fault, it certainly cost him a little trouble this time as I not-gently-at-all ripped Charles O'Shea the bartender out of his loving embrace and put the bastard through his own glass coffee table. His ashtray got caught up on the metal frame and followed a second later, delivering a nice thump and a load of nastiness to the back of O'Shea's head and leaving a knick on his scalp the length of my forefinger.

I dragged Charlie up and slammed him into the drywall with about a hundredth of the force and a millionth of the rage I had available on hand. His eyes squinted shut in pain, then opened just a sliver experimentally. "I'm still here, dipshit," I said, and rammed him into the wall again. Lightly, I swear. If he died of this, it'd be from embarrassment or an undisclosed heart condition, because these were my version of love taps. "I am not a figment of your imagination."

"What do you want?" Charles asked, two steps past panic.

"Not interior decorating tips," I said. I tried to decide if I should just steal his memories here, in front of everybody and ruled it out. I caught a knowing look from Zollers as he made his way over to lean against the wall so I could see him plainly even as I held Charles an inch or so off the ground against it. He knew what I was thinking, knew what I'd done, and knew I was ashamed of it. Partaking of someone's memories, their soul, it always felt like something dirty to me, like something I should hide from. I had an easier time knowing that there were pictures of my blurry, naked ass streaking across the skies of various cities where my clothes had been burned off in fights than coping with the idea that anyone would see me taking memories out of someone's head.

It was private, it was weird, and it was the last thing I had left that I didn't want to admit to anyone.

"He doesn't know anything," Zollers said, sparing me the awkward discomfort of reaching into Charlie Boy's mind to figure that out for myself. Dr. Zollers plainly didn't think reaching into minds was that awkward, but his method didn't result from inappropriately long and awkward touches that released a feeling inside me that was akin to—well, you know. In that regard, I felt way, way too close to the succubi of fiction, the ones that everyone in the press seemed super eager to lump me in with. Like an idiot with a hammer who saw nothing but nails everywhere, everything was about sex with these bastards. Put the hammer away, you dinks. "If you want," Zollers said, "I'll take him to the police in his car, let you two drive back to HQ on your own."

I let Charles go, frowning. "Why?" I asked, turning to look at him.

Zollers shrugged lightly. "Do you trust me?"

I started to smart off, then stopped myself. "Yeah."

He held out a hand, and I shoved Charles roughly toward him. As I did so, I saw a glazed look run over Charles O'Shea's face that told me he wasn't going to escape Zollers's custody of his own volition. "See you back there." Zollers smiled weakly, and Charlie walked behind him in perfect sync.

"Was that weird?" Augustus asked me, stepping up to stand at my side, scratching his head.

"Yes." We watched them go, and I shook my head, trying to figure out the next move. "We should ..." I couldn't stop shaking my head. "Go back, I guess."

"Yeah, all right," he said, shrugging. He was walking a little tentatively, and he led the way back to the car, one of the dark agency SUVs that we took everywhere. "You think you're gonna calm down anytime soon?" He looked at me sideways on that one.

"Sorry," I said as I made my way to the driver's seat and unlocked the door. I hated driving, but every time I suggested Augustus do it he called me Miss Daisy, another of his never-ending attempts at humor.

"You about ripped that guy out of my hands," he said, getting in the front seat of the SUV and slamming the door behind him as I did the same. "I mean, I'm just recovering here, thought I'm going out on some nice, light little detail where we go to brace some punk, and ..." He frowned as I started the car. "You know, we didn't even get anything out of that."

"I know," I said, sighing, letting my head slump forward a little. "We're on the wrong side of the email wall, here, chasing this guy and those assassins I got this morning. It's like there's a watertight compartment between us and the Brain, and—" I paused, catching a hint of something in the air.

"What?" Augustus locked eyes with me and must have seen the alarm in my face, because he started to look a little panicked, too.

"Watertight compartments can get busted open, too," said a voice from the back seat as I spun around to look at the young man waiting there, his glasses catching a gleam from the sunlight outside, his dark skin only a few shades off from the leather he sat upon. "You just need someone like me to make like an iceberg and do the work."

17.

"Jamal!" Augustus half-hissed, half-screamed, looking more than a little perturbed at his brother. "You scared the hell out of me! Who creeps into the backseat of a fricking federal agency car and just sits there? What if she'd killed you, scaring her like that?"

"Hey," I said, nonplussed. "I haven't even killed anyone yet today, and if ever there was a time for it—" I looked him up and down. "Also, I'm not the one who looks scared."

"Well, he startled me," Augustus said, more than a little nonplussed himself. Looking like he had a wicked case of the shakes, he rounded on his brother again. "What are you doing here?"

"Heard you broke your back," Jamal said, all cool. I didn't know him all that well, but he struck me as that sort of guy, calm almost all the time. I'd implicated him in a series of revenge murders that he'd performed down in Atlanta after the woman that he loved got killed by a criminal conspiracy, but he'd done the deed with lightning powers and brought an even bigger problem to light, so I'd let him skate.

Maybe I could sympathize with his plight a little. Or something.

"Well, my back got broken," Augustus said, "I didn't do the breaking myself, though." He frowned. "How'd you even hear about that?"

"Digital eyes everywhere, brother," Jamal said, looking

out the window. "Always watching."

"That's a little creepy," I said.

"It's a brave new world," Jamal said, leaning forward. "You know what kind of people it has in it?"

I squinted at him, trying to decipher his meaning. "All sorts. Which kind are you talking about?"

He licked his lips. "The kind that you can't get through the watertight wall into."

Augustus gave his brother a look. "Jamal, what are you doing here?"

"Well, I was in town to check up on you, little brother," he said. Jamal was probably a good five inches shorter than Augustus. "But I figured once I saw what was going on, I could lend a hand to someone who's in a situation not unlike one I'm familiar with."

"You want to help her get revenge?" Augustus asked, disbelief written across his face. "Haven't you done enough of that on your own?"

"Wait," I said, holding out a hand to get Augustus to stifle himself, "you want to help me?"

"If your enemies are throwing darts at you," Jamal said, pushing his lips together as he paused to let that thought sink in, "they're hitting other places on the board now. This Anselmo guy that came at Augustus, he was straight out of their camp."

"What do you know about all this?" Augustus asked, looking at his brother with a dose of skepticism strong enough to stun a bull elephant. "How much have you been watching?"

Jamal touched a finger to the door. A spark of electricity ran through, unlocking the doors with a sharp click that caused Augustus to jump. "I'm watching more than anyone else lately."

I pondered his offer, that cold fury that had been coursing through me only a few minutes earlier as I kicked down Charles O'Shea's door metamorphosing into something different, something I still couldn't describe, or maybe something I didn't want to. The layers of the cake were getting even more muddled. "What do you need?" I asked, and the only thing I could really identify was ... hunger. Desire to know.

"Take us back to your headquarters," Jamal said, nodding at the road ahead. "I need a computer and some time, and I'll open your eyes."

"Whoa," Augustus said, and he landed a hand on my arm. I eyed it and he pulled it back like he'd gotten burned. "You sure this is a good idea?"

"He's your brother," I said, putting the car into gear. "It'd be rude not to at least listen." And I pushed gently down on the accelerator pedal instead of slamming it to the floor like I wanted to, controlling my breath as I hurried to get us home, back to where I could finally get some answers.

18.

I stood watching Jamal do his thing from over J.J.'s shoulder, ignoring the workday noise of the agency's fourth floor as I waited for the results. The whole place had a quiet, placid feel to it, like the people who worked here hadn't quite recovered from the manhunt that had dragged so many extra hours of effort out of them. It was like someone had given them all a shot of sedation and they were just trying to keep from toppling over for a snooze right on the carpet between cubicles.

"How in the hell are you doing this?" J.J. asked in awe, adjusting his glasses as Jamal's fingers danced over the keys, presumably unlocking doors J.J. only wet-dreamed about.

"My power is over electricity," Jamal said, not stopping as he explained. "Most people who have that use it for bolts of lightning and such. I refined it over a couple years, figured out how to control 1's and 0's, even at a distance."

"Yeah," Augustus said with a distinct lack of enthusiasm, "you're a real badass. You're a nerdy, black Cole McGrath."

Jamal paused to look up at his brother. "And you call me a nerd, throwing out the name Cole McGrath like people should know who that is."

I'll admit it, I didn't have a clue. "Who's Cole McGrath?" I whispered to J.J., forgetting that the Colemans were both metas and could hear me.

"I understood that reference," J.J. said with pride, like a sunbeam was about to burst out of his chest. "These are my people." He paused as Jamal and Augustus both looked at him cockeyed, and J.J. thrust his hands up. "No! Wait! Not like that! Not what I meant!"

"I think I'm about to kill you all," I said, letting a little frustration bubble out. "Can we get on with—"

"Sienna!" Ariadne's voice cracked across the floor.

I controlled my spin, gracefully coming about with a faux smile on my face. "Yesssssss?"

Ariadne came into the cubicle, looking at me like I was being weird. Which I was. "What are you doing here?"

"I'm about to bust this case wide open," I said, glancing back at Augustus. He shook his head at me, clearly disapproving of me saying it like that. I toned it down and tried again. "Jamal was about to show us who's responsible for all my problems."

"What do you mean, responsible for all your problems?" She put her hands on her hips. "You cause more than a few of them yourself, like hitting a reporter—"

"Actually, this Brain sent those reporters to ambush Sienna," Jamal said helpfully. I was suddenly much happier I'd let him get away with murder. Uhhh … it sounds bad when I say it like that, doesn't it? "She's also been feeding reporters all sorts of bad info, rumors and stuff—"

"Yeah, yeah," J.J. said, all enthusiastic, like a dog looking for a pat on the head. "I figured that out, too, by tracing some of the fake IP addresses for the Brain and back-checking the emails accessed from those—"

"So the bottom line is that Sienna's been the victim of a lovely public relations tar-and-feather campaign," Augustus said, clearly losing patience with the geek speak.

"So you really didn't punch that reporter in the face?" Ariadne asked, not pulling her eyes off me.

Stark silence fell in the cubicle. "Well, no, I did," I said, "but there were extenuating circumstances! I was baited!"

"When have you ever required bait to hit someone who was annoying you?" Ariadne asked, looking at me a little warily.

"Hey," I said. "Do you not get this? This whole campaign of misery where the press turned against me since the prison break in January, it was all orchestrated, like ... like the Brain is a conductor," I said, barely finishing the analogy.

"Was Kat's release of your conversation on television orchestrated?" she asked, still looking skeptical.

I looked at Jamal, who shook his head silently. "No, that was just Kat being a—" I said.

HEY! Gavrikov shouted before I could deliver my unvarnished opinion. *That's my sis—*

"Oh, shut it, Aleksandr," I said, to the probable alarm of everyone around me. "Ariadne, don't you get it? A lot of this shit that's happened the last few months—it isn't my fault." I watched her for the light to go off.

She didn't exactly look bullet-hard, but she stared me down with a kind of sympathetic face. "And some of it is. I get that this lady has been shooting at your feet to make you dance, but ... you got to choose how you reacted to the things she did. For example, punching the reporter in the face."

"I didn't—what the hell? Let me shoot at your feet and see if you dance." Now I was getting annoyed. "I didn't choose to get hounded by them, I didn't choose to get poisoned by them, and I damned sure didn't ask for them to send the press up my ass for every little thing."

She looked a little wounded as she slinked back a step. "I've seen you like this before, you know."

I let out a hot breath of irritation. "No, you haven't."

"Really?" Her glance was all accusation. "Pretty sure I have. All pissed off and sure you know where to direct it. I seem to recall waking up to you kicking down a door—"

I blanched, and in my head Eve Kappler experienced a swell of self-righteous satisfaction. *She's right, you know.* "I'm not—" I took a breath, getting myself under control. "I haven't even killed anybody yet today," and even to me it sounded like a plaintive whine.

"I like how you throw in the 'yet,'" Augustus said, "covering your bases and all."

"You're too close to this one, Sienna," Ariadne said quietly. "You should back off, let someone else—"

"THERE IS NO ONE ELSE," I said, and swung my hand back hard enough to hit the cubicle wall and crack it, knocking the whole cubicle farm back six inches. "Don't you get it?" I stepped closer to her and she stepped back, eyes wide, stumbling slightly as she retreated. "I'm the only one who can do these things, can handle the threats. Who else are you going to send?" I whipped a finger at Augustus. "He'll be great in a few months, but he's just one guy, with one set of powers. What happens when you send him up against someone who can control water so well that they can knock his earth projections down into the mud? What then?" I shrugged my shoulders hard. "Reed? If he lives?" I spit it out caustic, like that chemical that Michael Shafer had thrown in my face last night. "Forgive me for not exactly being 'blown away' by his powers. He's good, but I could break him like a twig in two seconds." Ariadne was taller than me, but she was wilting under my verbal assault. "So who else you got? M-Squad's gone, Ariadne—"

"Because of you," she whispered.

"Because they crossed *me*," I said, still furious. "I'm it. They may call this the Metahuman Policing and Threat Response What-the-hell-ever, but they ought to just call it what it is—Plan A: We send Sienna Nealon to beat your ass if you step out of line, metas."

"Holy shit," J.J. stage whispered. "Cat fight."

I whirled on him. "Really? Really? Is it a cock fight when you argue with another guy? Or is it just arguing?" When he looked appropriately chastened, I threw the cherry on top. "Now stop being a little dick and let the women talk."

"Do you even see yourself right now?" Ariadne asked as I turned back to face her. Her cheeks were flushed, her neckline mottled red. "Can you hear what you're saying? You're not on an even keel."

"My boat's been turned over," I said. "By months and months of concerted effort on the part of the Brain to sink me."

"Not just her," Jamal said, reminding me he was there. "She's got accomplices."

I turned to look at his computer screen, which was basically just walls of text that I didn't understand. "Eric Simmons, you mean?"

"More than that," Jamal said, and pointed to one section of the text. "Your Brain's name is Cassidy Ellis. She's a meta," he pulled up a picture of a sullen girl in a mug shot, darker hair falling in wisps over her pale face. She looked like a teenager. "This is six years ago, last time she got arrested."

"What's her power?" I leaned in, looking into the face of my enemy for the first time. She looked as pissed at the camera as I was at her.

"She's an actual brain," Jamal said. "It's not exactly recorded, but based on what I've seen of her school records, her patterns, what I can catch off her computer, she's super-genius IQ."

"If she's so damned smart, why does she keep failing so hard at killing Sienna?" Augustus asked. I tried not to be offended at his insinuation that I was no intellectual match for an evil super genius.

"Girl could probably calculate pi to ten thousand spaces in her head—" Jamal started.

"Like Edward Nygma!" J.J. squealed. He looked contrite a moment later. "Sorry. Sorry. But you do know who Edward Nygma is, right?"

"Yeah, I got that one," I said, and turned back to look at Jamal. "So she's smart, but—"

"Rocket scientist smart," Zollers said, entering our

discussion quietly, stepping past Ariadne, "but my guess is that someone with an IQ this high doesn't have a clue about human emotion, how it affects the way we think, the way we act. She could put together a computer model that could predict the heat death of the universe down to the second, maybe even do it in her head, but she doesn't have the emotional intelligence to know why you'd be mad at her for what she's doing right now." He shrugged. "She lacks empathy. Utterly. It's all a computer game to her."

"Can you sense her?" I asked.

"No," he said, "but when you've been in as many minds as I have, you get a feel for these things. Some people are very intellectually capable but fall apart when it comes to interpersonal relationships. Others are excellent with emotion and human nature but would struggle to solve for x on the simplest algebra equation." He looked at me. "She's Wile E. Coyote, and can't figure out why the Roadrunner isn't getting caught in her perfect traps."

"But she's not alone," Jamal said, drawing my attention back to him yet again. "This address, the one she's staying at? It's just outside Omaha, Nebraska. Property's been registered to the same person for eighty years. Social security administration indicates that there are three people at this address, a mother and two dependents."

"Social security?" Augustus frowned. "So they're old?"

"The mother is," Jamal said. "I found a birth record that says she came into the world in Lancaster County, Pennsylvania in 1857. Amended later to reflect an 'error' in the original record and moving that date to 1957."

"She's a meta," I breathed, leaning in to see what I could from the wall of text.

"Her dependents are in their twenties," Jamal said. "They're listed as her grandchildren, with a deceased father. That was the reason for the social security checks. Survivorship income."

"Doesn't that cease at age eighteen?" Ariadne asked.

Jamal shrugged. "Something funny there. But whatever the case, they survived the death of their father and they're collecting his social security." He leaned in, squinting through his glasses. "Their names are Claudette, Denise and Clyde Clary, Jr." He turned his head to look at me, and I knew he knew.

"You make your own problems," Ariadne whispered behind me, and I didn't dare look her in the eye, because I knew, in this case, that she was right.

19.

Ma

It was a council of war they were having, but not the sort of council Ma wanted to have, and certainly not in her living room. At least Cassidy had dried herself off for this one first, and hallelujah for that. She sat her skinny ass on the couch, Eric Simmons cuddled in next to her, putting on a fine show. She didn't care for him or his city-boy beanie cap that looked like it'd been crocheted by some damned hippy, nor did she much like his long hair beneath it. He had soft features, and he'd made a great girl for somebody in prison.

"We need to regroup," Cassidy said, sniffling. The windows were open, and Ma knew that the smell of the outside caused the girl's allergies to flare up. It was a trick she'd used to her advantage wherever possible over the last few months, to keep the windows open as much as possible to force Cassidy to stay in the tank rather than annoy the holy hell out of her.

"We're pretty grouped right now, I'd say," Junior snickered. He sat on a chair dragged in from the kitchen table, clearly not wanting to share the couch with the lovey-dovey couple. Even Denise had moved to the recliner to put a little distance between herself and those two.

"Our plan failed," Ma said, finally inserting herself into the meeting. Cassidy would want to run the discussion, and

Ma was mostly fine with that, but she'd need to keep it on track, because Junior would devolve it into a discussion about body parts or farts or something of the sort given half a chance. "Time for a new one." She didn't even need to say that it was Cassidy's plan that had failed. The girl flushed in embarrassment at the oblique criticism without her even putting the edge on it.

"Those assassins you hired got caught, too," Denise said with a sour look. "What else we got?"

"They came recommended," Cassidy said with a hard breath. Her asthma would be acting up pretty quick. "I don't know that we can get our hands on any mercenaries or anybody else like that in short order. They're pretty in demand these days in Revelen for some reason—"

"I don't give a crap about that European bullshit," Junior said. "I just want to kill this girl, and then I want to settle in for football season. Is that so hard? The Cowboys got a good schedule this year." He had a resigned look about him, tired of the meeting already.

"Junior," Ma said gently, "you're excused."

"I'm not leaving until we sort this out," Junior said, giving her a little attitude. "This bitch was supposed to be dead already. How come lady genius can't even figure out how to kill one damned person?" He pointed at Cassidy.

Cassidy, predictably, flushed and answered with a sputter. "I couldn't account for her taking a prescription drug that wasn't in her medical records and that our man on the inside didn't even know about—"

"Why don't we just have this inside man shoot her in the back of the head?" Denise asked. She mimed making a pistol with her index finger. "Boom, dead. Problem solved and we can all get on with our lives."

"She needed to suffer," Cassidy said, still red, "for what she did to my baby in New York." She cuddled up with Simmons, who made an *awww* noise and pulled her closer. As soon as her head was tucked under his, he went from looking like he was preciously amused to slightly disgusted.

Denise didn't even bother to hide it. She turned her pistol finger back toward her own temple and feigned pulling an invisible trigger, then gagging herself with it. "I'm 'bout to be sick," she said, as though her action hadn't already made it abundantly clear.

"She needed to suffer originally, I agree," Ma said, stepping in to guide things again, "but we're past the point where we can afford to take that sort of leisurely revenge. The girl is stubbornly refusing to die, and all your plans to sink her by making her a pariah aren't bearing the kind of fruit we can eat. More like a damned green crabapple. She just needs to die at this point, clean and away from where it could implicate any of us."

"We can still make her suffer," Cassidy said, sitting up out of her baby's arms. "I can turn up the heat on the press thing. Give them some new blood."

Ma considered that one for a minute. "Look ... I think we all know that America looks for chances to eat its own, but we been chumming these sharks for months and they ain't figured out how to make her their dinner yet. She's not respected, we know she's about two steps from getting fired, but we can't seem to make that thing happen." Ma shrugged. "I think she's close enough. She doesn't even barely have any friends anymore. We know she cries at night. This thing's getting too hot for us. Let's just put her out of our misery already."

"Our inside man's not going to do that," Cassidy said with a shake of her head. "He's been clear, that's not in his job description, and it'll jeopardize his position."

"I'll shoot her," Junior said, blowing out a big ol' raspberry. "I'll get my rifle and just plug her in the back of the head."

Everybody looked at him, but only Simmons spoke. "What happens when she dodges at the last second, turns around and beats your ass to a bloody pulp?"

Junior didn't answer, but his skin glinted as he turned it to steel. "I'd like to see her try."

"Junior," Ma said carefully, "Sweety, she killed your daddy like that, and it was before she even had these new powers."

"I don't give a shit," he said defiantly, pissed out of his gourd, "I'll rip her into pieces and wipe my ass with her face."

"Oh, gross," Cassidy said, flinching away.

"You're a real class act, Clyde," Denise said.

"You're a real ass act, Denise," Clyde spit back, "now go shake it somewhere that they give a damn about yo' fat, jiggling—"

"Children," Ma said, taking out her stern voice. They both responded immediately, collapsing into a sullen silence. Cassidy sneezed in the background, and Ma caught a glimpse of her eyes watering heavily. "Yeah, I think we're past time we need to cut bait and get this over with." She looked at Cassidy, who was tugging free of Simmons. Not surprisingly, the man didn't look sorry to see her go. "Darling," she said, "why don't you start figuring out the best way to get someone close to her and we just shoot her and be done."

"All right," Cassidy said, heading for her tank, clearly distressed since she wasn't even bothering to argue for a smarter plan than "Shoot her." She opened the lid and climbed in without even stripping out of her clothes first. Ma smiled as the tank shut, the sound of the heat pump coming on as she locked herself in drowning out anything the girl might hear inside.

Simmons sprang to his feet, looking ready to leave again, when Ma gave him a slow smile that caused him to hesitate. "Eric, darlin', why don't you sit down for a spell?" He froze, and she could see the uncertainty spread over his face, and it only got worse when she hit him with the next part. "I think we need to have a talk about you being faithful."

20.

Sienna

There was something about a six-hour car trip in a crowded SUV that made me even ornerier than before I'd gotten in the car. Maybe it was Augustus and Jamal periodically picking at each other like brothers, maybe it was Zollers sitting in utter silence by the window, or maybe it was just Scott chattering in the driver's seat like it was business as usual, but it drove me bug-squat crazy.

"Oh, I see how it is," Augustus was saying. "Can't be bothered to make it in time when I'm injured by an invincible Italian, but Sienna has a redneck conspiracy to break her come up and you're suddenly in town, willing to help in like two seconds."

"I told you," Jamal said, "I came to make sure you were all right after your back got broken, but it takes kind of a while to get to Minnesota by bus from El Paso—"

Augustus tapped me on the shoulder, and I reluctantly turned around. "Do you believe this?"

"It's a war crime on the level of having a Nielsen box and watching the Kardashians," I agreed without much conviction as we bumped along a dirt path lined with stubby trees on either side that were rapidly losing their leaves. Reminded me of a man going bald but struggling to keep it combed over. Let it go with dignity, guy.

"What are we looking at here, again?" Scott asked. "Clyde Clary's pissed-off relatives?"

"Mom, son and daughter, I guess." I thumped my fingers against the plastileather interior features of the SUV. "No idea on their powers, Jamal?"

"Nah," he said from the back seat. "No record on these three that would indicate it. Clyde Jr.'s had some arrests, but never resisted, surprisingly." He paused. "That said, I did find another interesting thing about how the Council Bluffs police station suffered some unexplained damage about a month after he got arrested there one time. Looked like a wrecking ball went through the wall."

"I'm going to assume he's like dear old dad, then," I said, puckering my lips. "Changeable skin. He could be steel one minute, bone the next."

"Why wouldn't you be anything but steel all the time?" Augustus asked. "All invulnerable and whatnot."

"Clyde used to try different states when he was in therapy with me," Dr. Zollers said, staring out the window at the expansive fields beyond the trees lining the road's perimeter. "He had a difficult childhood and had exactly that view; I made him shift into velvet in order to show him a softer side of himself."

"It didn't take," I snarked. "Should have made him stay velvet for longer."

"He was a rough individual," Zollers said, finally turning his attention away from the window. "A little more rural upbringing, not a lot of tolerance for excess emotion. I got the sense his mother was ... manipulative."

"Any chance he mentioned if she had powers?" Scott asked. There was a split in the road ahead, two mailboxes parked right in the middle of the Y.

"I don't recall him discussing it, no," Zollers said. "He did talk about his children from time to time, though."

"I'm still amazed old Clyde had children," I said. "One, because—ew, that anyone would lay him, let alone twice, and two, because he was like twelve when he died." Well, he acted like he was twelve anyway.

"He was forty-six," Zollers said.

"Really?" I couldn't keep my mouth from falling open at that one. "God, what a Peter Pan complex on that guy."

"Looks like we're coming up on the second star to the right," Scott said, and I heard the tension in his voice as he angled the car to the right, where the mailbox was ... held on by bungee cords and with the name "Clary" written on it in bold white letters like they'd been freehand painted by a moron. Which, given the mental capacity of Clyde, Sr., the odds were good on.

"Do we stop here?" Scott asked, slowing the van to a crawl.

"No," I said, looking down the driveway. There were more trees lining the dirt path, and a couple ruts showing where everyone who'd come this way had driven, over and over. Beyond the trees were empty fields, flat ground, and at the very end of the road, a half mile or so in the distance, I could see a house. "Just step on it; we'll roll up and bust down the doors before they have a chance to respond." I blinked and looked back at Jamal. "You're sure they don't know we're coming?"

"I've put every traffic camera that could have revealed us into a loop, so as far as anyone knows, we're still at your HQ," Jamal said. "There's no way they can know we're coming."

"Then let's go kick down the door and end this," I said, feeling a hard resolve creep over me. These people had made my life hell for the last few months. *For you, Reed*, I thought. But there was a little nagging voice inside that told me it wasn't just Reed I was doing this for.

21.

Ma

"Someone's coming up the driveway," Junior said as they stood around Simmons, who was practically shaking on the couch. Ma had hit him with what they knew, and he'd reacted like all cheating cowards probably did, begging her not to tell, pleading that it was just that once, twice, three times with each lady. His face was all red and sickly, burning humiliation from forehead to chin. It hadn't taken long to get him to start confessing stuff she didn't even want hear about, liaisons he'd had in places she'd never even heard of. The man was a serial cheater, that was no doubt, and it was taking all her restraint not to just slap him out of the verbal diarrhea state he'd fallen into. By now he was just quivering and looked like he needed a smoke to calm his nerves.

"Well, check on it, will you?" Ma asked, rolling her eyes. "We're in the middle of having a conversation here."

"Yeah, all right," Junior said, clearly not happy about it. He strolled off with his wide-frame self toward the front of the house.

"Now, Eric," Ma said, leaning a little closer to Simmons, "here's what I want to know. It seems to me you don't really have a lot of loyalty to Cassidy over there." She waved her hand vaguely at the tank.

"No, no," Simmons said, shaking his head. "No, I love her—"

"Eric," Ma said, "you done slept with about eighty women by your own admission, and most of 'em since you got together with Cassidy." She exchanged a look with Denise, who seemed to be enjoying this all immensely. "I get that you like to make girls quake, but … let's just be honest. You're using her."

Simmons's mouth moved without words coming out, open and closed like a fish out of water. "No, I … it's not like that …"

"It's exactly like that," Ma said, doing her best Dr. Phil impersonation. "It's a problem of competing desires. See, Cassidy wants a faithful man, and you want to get your little dangle wet with every woman you've ever met."

Simmons furtively swept his gaze to Denise. "Not every woman."

Ma was about to slap the shit out of that boy when Junior came busting back into the room, hightailing like his rectum had just been lit like a fuse. "Sienna Nealon's coming up the driveway in one of those agency cars!" His eyes were wide and he didn't have that air of joking about him. "Got a bunch of her friends with her!"

"We'll kill her right now," Denise said, standing up abruptly. "Let's just do this—"

"No." Ma cut her off. She had more than a shiver of fear. "Cassidy didn't even see this coming, which means Nealon's tumbled to her little game." She looked at Simmons. "Your girlfriend's all played out. We're about to get caught in a bear trap, and she either didn't see it coming or she wanted to see us step in it."

Simmons was about two steps from panic. Clearly he hadn't seen it coming, either. "Wha … what do we do?"

Ma was a step ahead of him. She turned back to Junior, keeping her calm. "You said she's got her friends with her?"

Junior nodded. "Yeah, but …"

"All right," Ma said with a nod. "Here's what we're gonna do …"

22.

Sienna

Someone threw a car at our SUV and it hit head on, a collision that deployed the airbags and sent all of us smashing forward. I saw the movement before it happened, but I didn't get a look at who did it, hiding behind the car before they threw it. I also didn't manage to get out the door in time to stop it because I got tangled in my seatbelt and only managed to get halfway out the door before it hit. I smashed into the ground and was lucky in that the car didn't land on me, because that would have probably been at least as uncomfortable as a meteor on my shoulders. Really, when it comes to pain, your nerve endings can only register crushing pressure up to a certain point, and I doubt they differentiated between one ton of car and twenty tons of rock.

I lay there bleeding in the dirt for only a second, then sat up like the Undertaker. "Okay," I said, "someone's going to pay for that." I got up and looked into the SUV, where my little team was stirring. "Everyone okay?"

"Broke my glasses," Jamal said.

"Broke my asses," Augustus said, pushing his way out the door on his side.

"Feel like molasses," Scott said, continuing the rhyme pretty ineffectually as he pushed through a squeaking, protesting driver's side door to get out. "But I'm okay."

"We've got trouble ahead," Zollers said, tentatively getting out just behind me, rubbing his neck. "I'm getting ... strange readings out of a couple of them."

"What kind of strange?" I asked, hanging near the destroyed vehicle rather than charging ahead like a maniac— or my usual self, maybe.

"Like Clyde when he shifted forms. His mind wasn't clear when he changed." Zollers massaged his scalp; there was a small laceration at his hairline. "Looks like it's not just his son that has his power."

"Anything else?" I asked.

"Danger," Zollers said. "They're planning something."

"Any specifics?" Scott asked.

"They're at a distance, and the two people who aren't shifted don't know the plan," Zollers said, shaking his head. "Sorry."

"Let me go ahead and clear the—" I started, and then a rifle shot rang out, shattering my mirror and grazing my arm. I ducked, instinctively and drew my pistol. Augustus fumbled as he did the same, the only other person actually carrying a gun.

"That's not good," Scott said, hiding behind the open door of the SUV.

"Gotta be careful," I said, looking across two deflating airbags at him, "those aren't bulletproof—"

As if the shooter read my mind, another shot rang out and a spray of blood blew out of the side of Scott's neck. I watched his eyes widen, and his jaw drop as he scrambled to claw at his injury. Crimson spurted out from between his clutching fingers, and I watched the strength start to fade from his eyes as his life's blood ran down his fingers like water he couldn't control.

23.

Ma

"Got one!" Junior crowed from the front of the house. Ma was moving around, smashing her way through the walls where she knew the support beams were, not cracking them all the way through, but enough to get the thing ready. It was messy work, dusty, and it gave the air a cast as motes got caught in beams of light, stirred by the air as she moved.

"Good," she said. A face full of drywall dust hit her as she ripped a steel hand out with a wood stud clutched between her fingers. She smashed it to splinters and tossed it behind her, moving down the wall and repeating the process. "When she comes at us, we ain't gonna have much time, so you be ready to move."

Another gunshot rang out, and Junior cackled. "Got that bastard I already downed right in the back. She is gonna be pissed when he bleeds to death right in front of her!"

Ma didn't see it, but that didn't bother her at all. "Come on after us, Sienna. Come and get you some good ol' fashioned revenge."

24.

Sienna

"Scott!" I screamed, but he slumped to the side and fell to the ground, out of my sight, the first victim of this raid that I had brought about. I felt sick, and I knew in my heart that I'd screwed up again. He wasn't even supposed to be here. He'd left government service, had gone his own way into a profession where people weren't waiting to kill him because he was trying to lay the law upon them. But he was here because of me, because I'd started thinking like I used to, remembering the "good old days" when I'd had a team backing my plays, back in the war.

But this wasn't the war.

And I didn't need a team anymore.

Like Reed in the car explosion, these people were my vulnerability. They were my Achilles heel, and whoever was running things up in the Clary house knew it.

"Go!" Zollers urged from behind me as another rifle shot rang out, spanging off the metal on Scott's side of the car. "We'll take care of him."

I didn't need to be told twice. I zoomed into the air, out of view of whichever bastard Clary was taking potshots at us, up about fifty feet where I could spy down on the house without anyone being able to see me from inside. I hovered there like an avenging angel until I saw the muzzle flash from another shot. The crack of the rifle followed a second later, but I was already in motion.

I shot toward the origin of the gunfire and burst through the front door with a mighty kick. Normally, that sort of attack would have carried me through in a spray of splinters as I shattered the wood. And I did shatter it, but as soon as I did, I ran squarely into a solid wall and was halted in my flight path like I'd hit another meteor, head on.

I hit the ground after bouncing off, the wood floor cracking beneath me from the impact. The solid wall I hit took some of the momentum as well, a wide-framed, steel-covered man who looked awfully damned familiar even though I'd never met him before. He took a staggering step back from my hit, and the rifle flew out of his fat, steel-covered fingers as he moved to catch himself and ended up destroying a wooden shelf in the process.

I floated back to my feet as he recovered his balance and shouted, "Clear!" behind me.

"Ain't clear at all," Clary Jr. said, squaring his shoulders. The big bastard even sounded like his dad, ready to throw down right here. "'Bout to be a real stormy day for you, girl."

I clenched my teeth together. "Your dad used to call me that, and look where it got him."

I watched Junior's steel brow waver in fury. "'I'm a gonna kill you."

"'I'm a gonna' give you a lesson in grammar," I said, staring him down. There was a crashing sound at the rear of the house. I didn't know quite how to react to that, but it was far enough off that I didn't worry immediately. "Because apparently the public schools failed you in this regard."

"You're a superior sorta bitch, aintcha?" He scowled and revealed steel teeth that would have been the pride of ol' Michael Shafer himself. "Think you're better than everyone."

"Not so," I said, "just better than you and your scheming family of trash. You have to bring in a ringer just to do your thinking for you."

He swiped at me, but he was a little too slow, and I dodged. He tried to adjust, and I'll admit he was fast, but he ended up smashing an old couch to shreds in the process. "Hey, guy," I said, "you keep destroying your furniture and you're gonna end up raising the property values." He swung again and took out part of the plaster in the ceiling as I floated away. "Looks like this place could use a renovation anyway."

He started to come at me again, but a pile of earth burst through the nearest window and slammed into him like a battering ram, knocking him to the ground. The floor, already protesting under his weight, gave up and he disappeared through the boards into a basement cellar below, reminding me of a time his idiot father had brought a house in Des Moines, Iowa, down around our ears.

"Yeah," Augustus said, announcing his entry to the fray with a little gusto, "back to nature, mofo."

"You need a better tagline," I said.

"You got a gratitude problem, you know that?" he came up to stand by one of my shoulders while Jamal eased up to the other.

"I've got a lot of problems at the moment," I said, staring into the black hole in the floor as I floated back into the air. "I'll get right on that one once I've settled the hash of this Clary issue."

"You're going to be a while on that one, darlin'," came a woman's voice from the archway to my right. I spun and caught a glimpse of a lady with steel skin covered over by a big blouse and pants. She was rocking a body type just a little squatter than my own, her long hair turned to steel with her skin. She even had an apron on, leaving me no doubt who she was.

"You must be Clyde's mother," I said, staring her down. She did not look like she'd ever been intimidated by anyone, ever.

"They call me Ma," she said.

I passed on jabbing her with the fact that one less person called her 'Ma' now than did a few years earlier. "You've gone to an awful lot of trouble to make my life hell, Ma," I said instead.

"It hasn't been all that much trouble," she said, a flat statement of fact. "You make it pretty easy."

I didn't even know what to say to that. She wasn't smiling, malevolent evil, she wasn't cocking off like a quippy a-hole, she was just looking me in the eye and telling me that she wasn't sorry for putting me through the wringer. "It's easy to hit someone in the gut while they're already down."

"Now that depends on who it is you're hitting," she said. "You think you're going to make me feel bad about hitting while you've taken a knee? You took my boy from me. I wouldn't feel bad about ripping your guts out and feeding 'em to the dogs while you were watching it happen."

"Your boy held me down and made me kill someone I cared about." My voice was hoarse, and I couldn't have torn my gaze away from her if I had to. My skin was practically itching with the desire to pound the shit out of this woman.

"And you killed him in return," she said, ratcheting her anger up a notch. "Now I'm gonna put it to you. You know what we call that where I come from?"

"Suicide?"

"A feud." She didn't smile. "Blood for blood, an eye for an eye—"

"Looks like I'm going to come up short trying to get a tooth for a tooth, because you seem to be lacking—"

"Oh, I know how you must be looking at us," she said. "Clyde told me you thought he was just an ignorant hillbilly—"

"Your son was the dumbest muskox I ever met," I said. "He had all the brains God gave a centipede and none of the charm." I waved at the hole in the floor of her living room. "I see breeding won out." I tensed, ready to make my move.

"You think you're better than everyone," she said, "and

that's your weakness. You got a superiority complex that's gonna be the end of you."

"There's only one end you're gonna see here," I said, "and it's your own ass as you put your head between your legs and kiss it goodbye." I launched at her, and she reacted quickly, like I figured she would, throwing her own hands up to ward me away from hitting her. It was a common mistake from people who hadn't fought me, who didn't exactly know what I was capable of. I went right at her eyes to provoke that reaction, after all, and she did as expected.

I came to a stop in milliseconds, inches from her, and grasped her wrists. I yanked on them and started to spin, ripping her off the ground and spinning her like a hammer. It was my favorite move against bigger foes, because they never expected it from me. If I'd given her another second she probably could have countered by balling up and causing me to lose balance and drag her to the earth, but I released before she could, and she sailed through the roof of the kitchen, leaving a boulder-sized hole as she went about twenty feet into the air before she hit her apex and landed in a field.

"Hammer time!" Augustus yelled, and I shook my head at him. "Oh, come on!"

The floorboards exploded right then, and Junior re-entered the fray from below. He ripped down the floor near where he'd gone under, causing Jamal to scramble back, tossing a bolt of lightning downstairs as he did so. Augustus was in motion as well, jumping on a nearby stereo cabinet and clutching on like he was ready to climb it.

Clyde Junior jumped up to swipe at another bunch of floorboards, destroying a mass of his family's antique furnishings in the process and only succeeding in getting Jamal to move a little faster and throw a little more lighting. I was hovering above his influence and far enough away that he couldn't do squat to me, but I threw a few of Eve's light nets at him, the monster under the floor. He shrugged them off like I'd thrown a shot glass of water in his face. He looked more annoyed than anything, his steel face pinched.

Sienna! someone shouted in my mind, and it took me a second to realize it was Zollers. Clary Junior was destroying the house, heaving floorboards into the air with one hand as I pinned his other with a net of light, screaming frustration so loud that even the thunder of his footsteps on the cement floor were almost being drowned out. When I finally realized Zollers was speaking right to me, it was too late.

The entire house was shaking, and I didn't even know it until the first sections of the ceiling started to come down on top of me. The first piece of plaster was all the warning I got, because the whole damned thing followed a second later, Simmons' earthquake power coupling with whatever the hell Ma Clary had done to damage the house beyond its ability to hold together. Jamal, Augustus and Clyde Junior all disappeared from my sight as the roof came caving in along with the upper floor, dragging me helplessly down into the darkness as the world collapsed around me.

25.

Ma

"That's gonna leave a mark on somebody," Ma said as she dusted herself off. The landing hadn't been too rough, more disorienting than anything. Being in steel form didn't mean blood, bone and fluid didn't still exist in her body or inner ear, and being thrown through the air was dizzying, if not overly painful. She watched her house collapse in a pile of dust and mess, a cloud blossoming into the air like a low hanging storm as everything came down hard.

"You all right?" Denise asked as she squealed to a halt in the van. Ma turned her head to look and caught sight of Simmons hanging onto the side of the vehicle.

"Fine," Ma said, brushing herself off as the dust cloud hit. It wasn't much of one, but it left a little residue. She hauled the door open as it cleared and Simmons pulled himself inside the passenger door. "We just gotta wait for—"

An explosion of boards and plaster in the middle of the house wreckage caused Ma to raise an eyebrow. A steel hand shone in the sunlight, glinting like a mirror as it caught rays and reflected them. Junior pulled himself out of the rubble with a little effort, climbing up on the busted roof like he was getting out of a swimming pool.

"Get on over here!" Ma called, waving him down. He hesitated, and she fixed him with a look. "No argument now, let's go."

"You can't just leave her like this!" Junior called, but he was already heading her way. Slow, but doing it. "You wanted to finish it. We could finish it right now!"

"Or she could whoop you for a while and you could end up like your daddy," Ma called. She had a little quiver inside, knew the stakes on this one. Sienna Nealon wasn't someone she wanted to mess with when she wasn't ready for it. It wasn't like she was afraid to fight, she just liked to make sure her chances of winning were a little more certain than they looked at the moment. "Don't be stupid. You done hobbled her by taking out her support for a bit, don't screw it up by coming at her when she's mad as hell and has nothing else to lose."

Junior thundered across the open space between them and turned into rubber before he climbed in the van. The shocks still moved under his weight. Ma aped his move and did the same, slamming the van's sliding door shut as Denise floored it. Ma made a face; Junior had been smoking in here, and she hated that smell.

Simmons fidgeted in the front seat as the fields whipped by on either side. Denise was running the dirt road at close to sixty. Ma might have pushed it up a little higher, even though she didn't feel comfortable driving rough roads that hard usually. They bounced a little and she and Junior both hit the ceiling. "Shit!" he said.

"That's about right," Ma said as she came back down. She didn't mean the bump, of course. She meant losing the damned house she'd had for however many years. She couldn't even count 'em all anymore.

"Where we going?" Denise asked as they came up on a turn in the road. She went left even before her mother answered.

"Seems to me we find ourselves in a feud," Ma said, looking over Simmons's shoulder in front of her. The boy didn't look too good, but then, she'd just forced his loyalty pretty hard. "In a case like this, when you're facing down more than you can handle on your own, I find it's always best to turn back to family." Denise gave her a nod. She knew where to go, where to find the help Ma was looking for. The help they'd need to finish this thing up for good.

26.

Sienna

I watched ambulances carry Scott and Jamal away from the Clary house with a deeply sick feeling inside. Especially with Scott, as I watched the paramedics struggling to keep him from bleeding everywhere, I couldn't suppress the guilt, welling up inside me like the red that was now oozing almost uncontrollably from his neck. Dr. Zollers had staunched it until his healing had kicked in, but a secondary shot to his shoulder when he'd already been on the ground had made it much worse.

Jamal had just been knocked unconscious by a falling beam in the house collapse, but watching them wheel him away with his eyes closed and blood trickling out of his nose had been hard by itself. When you added the look on Augustus's face, also bloody, I might add, as the paramedics closed the doors on him and his brother, it was almost unbearable.

"This wasn't your fault, Sienna," Dr. Zollers said as the red-flashing lights faded into the distance, the boxy ambulances rocking on their suspensions on the uneven dirt road.

"I'm getting pretty sick of that patently false refrain." I stared after them for a minute and then cast a look back at the fallen house and the half dozen police officers that were standing around, not really sure what to make of the whole scene. At least they'd accepted my ID as a federal officer without getting all up in my face. They seemed to give me a wide berth, actually. "This was one hundred percent my fault," I said. "This entire thing, from the Clary clan to Eric Simmons, is all down to me."

Whether his powers were telling him to keep quiet or he just knew me well, he did not respond.

"If I hadn't killed Clyde Clary," I said, shaking my head, "none of this would have happened. And as for Simmons—"

"If only you'd let him get away clean with robbing the Federal Reserve," Zollers said, and here he was smiling slightly, "maybe his girlfriend might have decided to leave you be?" Now I didn't know what to say. "You're looking for ways to blame yourself," he said, "looking for ways to justify your withdrawal from humanity."

"I'm death, Doc," I said, gesturing back at the destroyed house, "you can't tell me being a little isolated isn't good for everybody."

"It'd be terrible for everybody," he said, serious as he could be.

I didn't quite do a double take. "How do you figure?"

"Who was the last person that had power like you and no connection to humanity?" Zollers asked, a little more coy than he needed to be.

I blinked a few times. "Sovereign? You think Sovereign became who he is because he—what, didn't have any friends?"

"Sovereign was so withdrawn from humanity, so detached," he said, "that he might as well have been a different species. He didn't view himself as one of us, not really. Not meta or human. He was 'a man apart' by his own admission. He wanted to create a better world for us, like a benevolent deity smiling down on his subjects."

"Being one of the people he wanted to create that world for," I said, staring at the wreckage of the house, with the roof cracked in three specific segments, "I remember all too well what his benevolence felt like. But that wasn't just from being a recluse for a while. I mean, he had other issues."

"He had limitless power and no accountability from normal people, people he could he listen to, whose dreams he could hear, whose fears he could taste," Zollers said, looking at me with those warm eyes. "He wanted to change the world, but the way he wanted to do it wasn't by leading; it was by crushing all opposition. He lost touch with humanity, especially the humanity of those who he perceived as standing in his way. He wanted to kill every single guardian of the old order because he didn't see them as people anymore." He straightened up and brushed the dust off his shirt, making a small cloud in the air between us. "When you withdraw from humanity, you cut yourself off from your own in some way, and when you've got amazing power coupled with it, suddenly you're convinced you're the impartial observer with all the answers, and why can't you just fix the problems? It's in your hands, after all."

"Sounds like a long road from there to here," I said, looking away from him.

"Because you never take aim at a problem and go forth to solve it without worrying about the consequences to yourself?" I turned around and caught him smiling, though faintly now. "It's always closer than you think."

"Uh, ma'am?" A cop's voice interrupted my opportunity to contest Zollers's assessment, and I turned to see a young guy in full uniform with a military style haircut waiting tentatively, like he was afraid I'd turn him into a toad or something.

"Yes?" I asked, probably a little higher than my normal conversational tone. It's like when you're in an argument with someone and you try to pretend you're not. I probably wasn't fooling anybody, least of all the young cop in front of me.

"We've got something over here you should see," the cop

said, and I followed him around the house as Zollers came with me, looking a little mysterious. We passed a crushed-in corner of old white paneling that probably hadn't been replaced since the turn of last century judging by the peeling paint, and moved behind the house where part of it was still kindasorta standing. In the back, the floors hadn't taken as much damage as they had where Clyde Junior had crashed through, so the walls had just fallen in, leaving a room at the back—well, not intact, but with the roof collapsed in and the wreckage still above ground.

No one had started excavating yet, which seemed wise given the structural integrity of the place was suspect at best. I paused at the back wall, folded neatly in half where it had dropped in on the room and listened, hearing something faintly tapping somewhere inside. "What the hell?" I asked.

"It's a surprise," Zollers said, still coy.

"Great," I said and seized hold of the back wall at the corner. I waited for the young officer and Dr. Zollers to step clear, and then I lifted into the air and ripped it up, tossing it into the middle of the wreckage pile that had once been the Clary household. I revealed what looked like a room that had partially sunk into the ground, the floor collapsing downward and threatening to spill everything into the fallen middle of the house like a black hole had formed to drag everything toward it.

I paused as the pieces I'd just thrown settled and listened again past the raised voice of the cops who were surprised by my little feat of strength. That same tapping came again from just in front of me, and I peered into the cloudy darkness of the collapsed room until I located its origin.

There was a cylindrical thing in the corner that looked kind of like a coffin or a photon torpedo from *Star Trek*, but bigger. It was bulky as hell and it took me a second to realize there was something—no, someone—inside making the noise. "Huh," I said.

"It's a sensory deprivation tank," Dr. Zollers said,

answering my question.

"A whut?" the officer asked.

"It's filled with salt water and insulated against outside noise so that someone can remain inside, afloat with nothing but their thoughts," Zollers said. "They were quite popular for a while."

"Lemme get this straight," the cop said, "you're saying there's someone in there right now. Someone locked up in there with—like a bunch of salt water."

"Yep," I said, smiling for the first time since this whole damned raid had begun. I grabbed the tank by its end and hauled it out of the wreckage of the Clary house as the room shifted behind it, the roof collapsing in as I removed one of its supports. Once the tank was out in the light of day, I reached for the handle and tugged on it. No dice.

I went around to the other side and ran a flaming finger down the two hinges, melting them to slag. Then I settled myself and yanked hard, tossing the metal top into the air behind me. It went flying off and dragged three flat-paneled computer monitors with it. They made a hell of a racket as they came to their landing.

"Whhhhaaaaat—" the officer said as I crept up on the tank, looking inside.

And there she was. Pale as her mug shot, eyes closed against the harsh light of day, hands up and trying to protect her face from that which was bound to assail her. She adjusted a little, enough to blink them open and see me, and I got the feeling she'd known I was the one pulling on her tank by the lack of reaction when she saw me.

"Hello, Cassidy," I said, probably just about leering at the small, thin stick figure in the tank. "I think it's time we had a meeting of the minds."

27.

It took all my restraint not to bust Cassidy's face into a messy, bloody pulp right there in the Nebraska dirt, or to just pop her like a zit right there in the salt water solution that smelled like there might have been a little pee in it. I dragged her out of the tank screaming and flailing her pale, scrawny limbs. She was wearing something like a one-piece bathing suit, and I hauled her up as she writhed.

"Holy mercy—" the cop nearest me said.

"I'll take it from here," I said and caught Dr. Zollers's eyes before twisting my grip on Cassidy even tighter and lifting her straight up into the air with me as I took off.

She screamed and screamed and screamed as I carried her higher and higher, trying to writhe out of my grasp as though she had a death wish. "You might want to simmer down," I told her helpfully as I got her up to about five thousand feet, "because I'm not sure you can survive a fall from this height, and my grip's not exactly infallible, knucklehead, especially after the shit your friends just pulled."

She stopped squirming and stiffened up. She didn't say anything, just hung there in her swimsuit onesie. I suspected she'd already run the percentages in her head and knew she wouldn't survive impact if she broke loose. I also didn't fancy her chances of survival if she expected me to catch her after tearing her way out of her swimsuit, because I'd have to grab her wet, slippery skin with my bare hands and get her to the ground before my powers caused me to absorb her soul.

I'd just maneuvered Ms. Super Smartypants into a no-win scenario, and she damned well knew it.

I flew her out to a freshly mowed field with nothing around for miles in any direction and swooped down, dropping her squarely in the middle of an exposed patch of tilled earth. The air was already turning cold around us, and when I dropped her I knew it was going to sting a little. I was cool with that, and she obliged me with a cry as she landed. Not hard enough to break anything, but hard enough to knock the wind out of her.

I doubled around and came flying back for effect, looming over her as she tried to get to her feet. "How fast can you run, Cassidy?" I asked, letting my mood cloud my face darkly.

She plopped back down on her skinny ass, black dirt all over her wet legs. "Not fast enough," she said with a sullen scowl of her own. It looked like the mug shot all over again.

"Your friends left you behind," I said, playing a hunch. "Did your boyfriend even tell you he was going to collapse the house?" Her sullen face wavered, and I knew in that moment that Zollers had the measure of her. All the brains in the world, not enough emotional maturity to handle a rebuke from a stranger. She pulled her knees close and wrapped her arms around them, still dripping beads of water onto the dirt. "He left you, did you know that? Ran off with the entire Clary family without even a word of warning."

She pulled her knees tighter to her chest, like she could put a wall between us. I felt a cool satisfaction roll through as my jab hit home. Her lower lip quivered as she tried to hold it together. This was the girl who'd tried to get the inmates in my prison to rise up and murder me, the person who'd been feeding my secrets, my sadnesses, my personal emotional tragedies to the press for months in order to prey on my insecurities.

"He abandoned you," I said, easing closer to her. I was

careful not to get too close, not because I feared for anything she could do to me, but because if she took a swipe at me I'd probably break her hand on general principle. "He left you behind the moment things got tough."

"You're lying," she said, shaking slightly. "We didn't even know you were coming."

"Oh ho ho," I laughed. "He didn't even have to pick between you and saving his own skin; Clyde Junior shot at me for five minutes before I made it in the door." My jaw tightened as I remembered the blood flooding out from between Scott's fingers. "He left you behind because he didn't want to take you with him. Ma busted the house's supports out while Junior distracted us, and Eric waited out back until she told him to drop the place around our ears with a custom-made earthquake." I moved to look her right in the eyes as she turned her head to avoid me. "Face it. He left you behind ... because he wanted to."

She shook her head back and forth in a tight, almost muscle-spasm driven way. Her eyes were fixed open and red, the tears already starting to stream. I blinked and looked at her, my surprise escaping before I could restrain it. "Is that ... are you ... crying? There's no crying in super villainy."

That got her to look right at me with those puffy eyes. Her lip quivered. "I'm not the villain. You are, and you don't even realize it."

"I'm the villain?" I pulled back my hand and put it on my chest like I was offended. "If I was the villain, Cassidy, I would have ripped the thoughts I needed out of your swelled head and left your carcass in the middle of this field for the crows to have a meal that fit their diet plan." I lurched toward her and she cowered away.

"You're the strong," she said, voice oozing contempt, "I'm the weak. You prey on the weak, it's what you do."

"I enforce the law," I said, feeling a little burn inside. "You and your boyfriend tried to rob the biggest bank in the country, in case you forgot, and then Simmons crashed a commuter train full of people in a vain attempt to escape the consequences of that act. He put the lives of innocent people at risk to save himself from jail. You're Bonnie and Clyde, if you're self-aware enough to recognize that makes you nothing more than petty, two-bit losers and not Hollywood-glamorized martyrs to the cause."

"I know what I am," she said, and turned her head away like she was denying me a kiss or something, "and I know who you are, and I'm not telling you anything."

"I never needed you to," I said, "and you know that." I stood up and loomed over her pitiful frame as she quaked in my shadow.

"You're going to enjoy this, aren't you?" Her voice shook a little, but she refused to look at me.

"More than you know," I said.

"You're a psychopath," she whispered. "You like to hurt people. You like to kill people."

"I'm neither going to hurt you nor kill you, Cassidy," I said, and grabbed her by her onesie as we both lifted off into the air. She let out a squawk of surprise as we surged back up to five thousand feet and I hit a cruising pace that was only a couple hundred miles per hour, well below what I was capable of. I didn't want to strain her swimsuit, after all. If I splattered her all over the countryside, it wouldn't achieve anything but fill the air with her screams for a few seconds before she came to an abrupt stop at the bottom.

"What the hell are you doing?" she cried out.

"I'm taking you to jail," I said as the wind whipped past my face and I headed north and east, toward the darkening sky. "Where you'll get to spend the rest of your life thinking about what you've done."

"You—you were supposed to take my memories!" she shouted. "You were going to—"

"You don't know anything," I said, firmly convinced I was right. "I don't need to read your mind to know that your friends betrayed you and didn't even give you a clue about where they were going."

Even in the looming haze, I could see her redden in fury. "I know more than you think I do."

"Twice as much, I'm sure. Maybe even three times as much, but unfortunately for you, thrice zero is still zero."

I flew on into the approaching night slowly, and the whole way back to Minnesota I got the satisfaction of watching Cassidy burn in silence—and I didn't even have to use Gavrikov to do it.

28.

Ma

The house was outside Council Bluffs, Iowa, just across the state line from Omaha, but it might as well have been across the world for Ma's purposes. They'd skirted the edge of civilization, watching the skies all the while, worrying that Sienna Nealon might coming swooping down from above at any moment. Well, Junior, Denise and Simmons had worried about it, anyway. She hadn't so much as cast a look in concern.

"Ma," Junior said, taking a break from looking out as they thumped up the driveway to the old house, "why ain't you worried?"

"The girl's suspended," Ma said, certain as she could be. "And we know what she's dealing with. She's got no access to anything at this point."

"Well, she found us somehow," Junior said, raising a decent point. "You don't think she can drone strike us or something?"

Ma pondered that. "You got a point there. Could be that computer geek figured out a way back to us. Cassidy wasn't nearly so smart as she thought she was, I reckon, being as she got caught flat-footed. But we stayed off the main roads, took the long way around, not a camera in sight and none of us have a cell phone, so …" She shook her head. "If she's gonna get us, she's gonna get us. We'll make our stand here, and this time we won't run."

"If that's way the way it's gonna be," Junior said, and she knew he was resolved now. Moment of weakness passed, he threw open the van door and got out.

Ma followed, hanging by a nervous Simmons. The boy looked washed out. "Just relax yourself, Eric," she said, and put a meaty hand on his shoulder. He quailed at the touch. "You just stick with us for a bit, and when we get all done with this, you'll be knee deep in some pretty little stick figure on the coast before you know it."

"Do the girls out there really have more plastic parts than a Barbie?" Junior threw out.

Simmons just blinked at him as they walked toward the front porch. "Uh …"

"What the hell are you doing here?" The voice was all challenge, greeting them from the porch. "Ma Clary over here in Iowa, as I live and breathe." The man who stood there wore overalls, the stereotypical sonofagun. He looked like a farmer even though he damned sure wasn't. "Never thought I'd see the day your clan came a callin' again, not after last time."

"Y'all don't know how to do a Christmas dinner, Blimpy," Ma fired back. His name was Dirigible Jim Clary, but everyone had called him Blimpy since he listened to the Hindenburg go down on the radio and jumped around like a maniac. His parents hadn't even named him until then. His mother was human and from the old school, when infant mortality was so high you didn't give a kid a name until they hit two; made it easier to part with them if you didn't get too attached. "You don't even think about having a squabble until after everybody gets fed."

"That was all on your boy," Blimpy said. He wasn't fat, that was for sure. Looked like he had wrought-iron limbs under his overalls. "He picked that fight, and I finished it for him." Blimpy turned and opened the screened door, shouting inside. "Janice! Buck! Get out here! We got kin come to visit."

Ma took the lead, sauntering up to the bottom railing of the porch. "Sorry to come calling out of the blue."

"It ain't a problem," Blimpy said as the door flapped open to admit a boy who would have been more aptly named if he'd been Blimpy instead of Buck. Buck wore a stained t-shirt with a Coca-Cola logo on it, holes all around the armpits to give a beautiful view of stray hairs sticking out. He didn't have a single one to spare on his head save for the sides, but he certainly had plenty to stick out of the armpits of his t-shirt. "Just so long as you didn't come looking to finish up that brawl. How long ago was that?"

"Eight years," Ma said. She threw out an arm and thumped it again Junior's arm as he stopped at her side. "Junior here was just a boy, didn't even have his power yet."

"No, nor did Denise," Blimpy said, eyeing the girl. "What are you now, girl?"

Denise didn't answer, but her hair shot out and hung in front of Blimpy who eyed it in surprise before grasping it and giving it a shake like it was a hand. "Medusa, huh? Well, all right then. Didn't know we had any of your kind in the family."

"Comes from her mother's side, I think," Ma said. "Listen, Blimpy, we got a problem." Janice brushed through the door behind her dad, looking like hell, hair out in every direction. That was the nice thing about being a Medusa, Ma supposed; she never saw Denise looking like that.

"What kinda problem?" Blimpy asked, pausing and spitting off the porch. He got a distance with it.

"We got a feud with the feds," she said. "We went after the one that killed Clyde—"

"Huh," Blimpy said, spitting again, "I told him before he went off to that job that it sounded like a government deal."

"Well, Sienna Nealon was the one that killed him," Ma said, "and now we got a feud with her. She wrecked our house."

Blimpy calculated that about a second. "Well, come on in, then."

Ma nodded as he opened the door. "You sure?"

Blimpy looked at her shrewdly. "You think I don't know what it means, opening the door to you? You got a feud with a federal officer. I know damned well what it means." He leaned toward her. "But you know what else I know? All the stories my daddy told me about the days when gods could damned well do what they wanted, when power was the ticket. Way I see it, that Sienna girl, she's the—whaddyacallit—the last bastion, the refuge of that agency—she's all they got, is what I'm saying." He smacked his lips. "I reckon we take her out, times are gonna be changing around here." He tugged his door open a little more and Buck made way, stepping off to the side. "So come on in … let's talk about how we go about ending this feud." And they did.

29.

Sienna

I came barreling into headquarters with my prisoner twisted up in my grasp. Cassidy had taken the moment of our landing as an opportunity to throw a shit fit, probably because she knew there were security cameras all around the lobby just waiting to capture her temper tantrum and the Sienna-clubbing-a-baby-seal reaction that would likely result. That film would sit in an archive somewhere, waiting for her or someone affiliated with her to someday hit it with a Freedom of Information Act request, and who knew, maybe it'd even be granted. We'd been lucky in that regard so far.

But I could see how she probably pictured it, and it had all the makings of being the next great YouTube hit video. Because it'd get millions of hits, plus the one where I knocked her unconscious and dragged her insensate body to her cell.

Rogers wasn't on duty now. Instead it was two guys, neither of whom I recognized. I suspected we'd suffered another mass culling of security personnel while I'd been comatose recently, but I hadn't had anyone confirm it for me. I was suspended, after all, so informing me as department head probably wasn't high on their priority list.

"Hi," I said, dragging Cassidy screaming across the floor. She was bucking her back against the tile, thumping her skinny ass up and down. "Got another one."

The two guards looked at me like I had toilet paper stuck on the bottom of my shoe instead of a slightly damp, pale-as-milk skinny Minnie in tow. Her butt was actually making sucking sounds against the tile floor as I dragged her up to them. Her onesie was strong, and I was thankful for this, since she was clearly the biggest infant on the planet at the moment.

"Uh ... we can't take that," the one on the left said, clearly speaking for both of them in this matter.

"You might want to," I said, "she's a federal fugitive, wanted in connection to the jailbreak that took place here in January." Just threw that out there, waited to see what effect it had.

The guards looked at each other, clearly not super happy about being in the middle of this. They cradled their M4s for comfort. Or something. "We, uh ... you know what? The boss is on his way down," one of them finally said.

"Oh, good." I twisted tighter on Cassidy's onesie as she bucked against the floor and screamed. "We'll just wait for him to get here, then." The two guards stared at her as she continued her toddler act. "So," I said, making conversation, "how's things? Enjoying your jobs so far?"

The one who'd spoken earlier looked like he was in a trance, watching Cassidy. The other looked right at me. He was middle-aged. His nametag said "Thorsen." "Been quiet up till now," he said, looking back to Cassidy as she tried to roll face down and punch the floor. "You know, my two-year-old does that when he gets really mad."

I nodded sympathetically. "How do you handle it?"

"Just ignore it," he said, shrugging. "Sooner or later they quit."

"She's not doing this for us," I said, "she's doing it for the cameras." I sensed Cassidy as she stiffened like a board. Apparently her emotional immaturity extended to having her plans foiled as well.

"What the hell is this?" Andrew Phillips asked as he strolled into the lobby. Cassidy had stopped with her fit and was now playing dead.

"I found your brain," I said to Phillips as I noticed a man in a tactical black ops type uniform, complete with ski mask, trailing a few feet behind him. "I mean, not yours, obviously, since I'm still fuzzy on whether you even have one, but *the* Brain—the one behind the prison break your first week."

Phillips kept his distance and his lurking shadow did the same. Phillips eyed Cassidy like she was a puddle of manure that was slowly seeping in under his door. "How do you know?"

"Magic," I snarked. Phillips looked at me with those dull eyes. "I backtraced her to a safe house outside Omaha where I caught her with Eric Simmons and some ... old friends."

"What kind of old friends?" Phillips asked, almost sounding like he was interested.

"A family by the name of Clary," I said, a little grudgingly. Phillips was a hell of a poker player; his eyes moved only slightly at the mention of the name.

"Huh," he said. "So ... are they the ones responsible for your little acid trip?"

"Seems so," I said. "But more important to our current discussion, she masterminded that incident that made you look like an ass on week one, so ..."

He gave me a hard look as I watched him think it through. "You're still suspended," he said, then jerked his head toward the door to the prison. "Let her in."

"Thanks," I said and started dragging Cassidy again as Thorsen the guard opened the door for me. A less gracious person might have pointed out that lately I'd been doing my best work while suspended, i.e. Chicago, but whatevs, man. He was unlikely to listen in any case.

"You should take that vacation you planned," Phillips called after me.

"I keep trying," I said as Cassidy launched into full

tantrum again, hammering the floor as I dragged her bodily to jail, "but these assholes just won't give it a rest." The door closed behind us, and Cassidy's wails of infantile stupidity echoed in the small room as I waited to put her in a cell again, but this time for good.

30.

I checked J.J.'s cubicle on the fourth floor and found it empty, with no hint when he'd be back. I opened the doors to every conference room and the supply closet where he'd once hidden during an attack without any luck before conceding he was probably done for the evening. I thought about calling him, but had to face facts—he was no Jamal, and by this point his brain had to be exhausted to the point of near uselessness. That didn't meant I couldn't drag some use out of it, but I'd just forced the Clary family to destroy their own house in order to save themselves from me. I didn't perceive them to be an immediate threat. I mean, even if they were going to drive from Omaha to here, it was going to take a few hours.

And I didn't feel like they were in that position when I'd parted ways with them. They were running away for a reason, after all. Running scared, running blind, trying to get away from me and—I suspected—trying to avoid the grid, which they knew was like a net that would entrap them.

They weren't stupid. Coming straight at me, barreling up the highway in a van that had registered license plates, that'd be running right into the net. I went to J.J.'s cubicle and did a little of the type of computer work that it always surprised people I knew how to do. Everyone thinks of me as a world-class ass-kicker, forgetting that I've got other skills. I was co-head of the damned agency for years, and I didn't just sit in an office that whole time.

I issued a BOLO—"Be on the lookout for"—warnings with state and federal law enforcement agencies, flagged Claudette "Ma" Clary, Clyde "Junior" Clary, and Denise Clary, and updated Eric Simmons's information to reflect his new "Known Associates." Ma Clary was clean as a whistle, but Junior had a record and so did Denise, though hers was for petty beefs like shoplifting. One of the police reports attached to her name had a store employee swearing she lifted items using her hair, which told me a little more about her.

Medusa-types could use their hair like a weapon, exerting control over it the way others could use elements. It was a weird power to watch in use, and one I'd only run across a couple times.

So, I had an earthquake maker, two stoneskins and a Medusa after me. If it came down to it, I could kill them all, of that I was fairly confident.

Still, I felt a nervous ripple through my stomach, one that wasn't helped by the sound of a familiar voice coming through my office door. "Aren't you still suspended?"

I looked up, ready to give whoever had said it a big, fat piece of my mind with some cherry syrup on top (I make it sound way better than it would actually be). And then I forgot all about it in an instant, because the person who was standing at my door …

… was Reed.

31.

He looked like hell and I told him so. His beard and long hair were gone, burned away in the fire and leaving behind red, angry skin in their place.

"Thanks," he said, sliding into my office a little gingerly, like he still hurt, though likely not from my friendly jab. He hesitated before speaking again, and I suspected it was not from pain. "I heard you haven't killed anyone yet."

I froze, looking at him like I'd got caught doing something bad instead of something ... uh ... good, right? "Who told you?"

"Ariadne," he said, clutching at his side like he had a broken rib. He could have. "Why do you look like I just accused you of murder?"

"Because I haven't killed anyone," I said, back a little stiff. "I haven't killed anyone for you, specifically. I mean, I should have been murderously angry, throwing vengeance and blood left and right, but instead—"

"Oh, you don't have to go wiping out the plagues of humanity on my account," he said, slipping down into one of the chairs in front of my desk. He looked deeply uncomfortable as he did it, and it didn't subside once he got settled, a grimace plastered across his lips. "Far be it from me to suggest you should go massacre people just because I got my car blown up." His discomfort turned to pursed lips of anger. "Though I am more than a little pissed about Baby.

Not sure car bombings are covered under my insurance."

"I think people are surprised I haven't left a trail of carnage," I said, leaning back in my chair. "Maybe I am, too. But the question I keep asking myself is … am I holding off on killing them because it's the right thing to do? Or because I'm afraid of what happens when it comes out?"

"You never worried about it before," Reed said breezily.

"I've never been this deep in the shit before," I said. "That reporter that ambushed me? The one I decked?" He nodded, and I went on. "He quoted me my unfavorables, like I was a political candidate. Asked me why President Harmon hasn't fired me."

"Ouch," Reed said, looking like he meant it all the way down to the bottom of him. "Why do you think you haven't been fired?"

I shook my head. "Like I told you in that conversation before we were so rudely interrupted by a car bomb … I think it's coming. It's in the wind, this idea that I can't keep running things the way I have and expect to keep a job. And up 'til now, Cassidy's been gunning for me, so I haven't gotten a fair shake—"

He frowned. "Who's Cassidy?"

"The Brain," I said. "You, uh, mighta missed a couple things while you were sleeping."

"You caught the Brain?" Reed sat up, then blanched in pain. "Owww. But good. But also … owww."

"I missed Simmons and company," I said. "Found out their accomplices, though."

He held very still. "Who?"

"The Clary family," I said, and watched his lack-of-eyebrows surge north. "Of Omaha, Nebraska."

"Uff-dah," he said, very Minnesota. "So that's why the Brain hasn't exposed your past misdeeds to the public."

I froze. I hadn't even considered that. "They never leaked the murders of M-Squad because—"

"It'd tie the Clary family to you in a public way," Reed

said, smirking a little. "Not the sort of thing you want to publicize if you want to get revenge on someone."

I slumped forward, putting my forehead on my hands. "I didn't even see it. It's like the dog that didn't bark."

"Yeah," Reed said. He held his silence for a minute before approaching a subject he clearly wasn't comfortable with, based on his tone. "You made them, you know." I tasted bitterness on the back of my tongue, and I didn't want to look at him. He went on anyway. "The way you went about things. You made more enemies for yourself."

"Ariadne beat you to this punch, and if you quote Tony Stark and say I created my own demons, I will hit you right in your Marvel fanboy broken ribs—"

"Yeouch," he said preemptively.

"Fine," I said, still looking down at the blotter on my desk. "I started it. But I'm gonna end it, too."

"How?" I could hear the genuine curiosity trickle through.

KILL THEM ALL, Wolfe shouted in my head.

Make it bloody, Bjorn offered helpfully.

Like a vengeful goddess, striking down all who oppose you, Eve Kappler added. I was only, like, 80% sure she wasn't being ironic.

"Death ends things pretty definitively," I said without much feeling.

"Yeah," Reed said, and the leather squeaked as he leaned forward. His words became a little more strained. "It's how you started it, too, though, with Clyde."

"Clyde started it," I said, and now the feeling crept in, dangerous, that fury that had been all the way in the back of my mind, not up front and exposed like a nerve. "He—"

"I know what he did," Reed said gently. "All I'm saying is, you do what you just suggested, and where does it end? What if more come? The Clary family—I dunno, cousins or something? The Brain's mother? Will you kill them, too?"

"Maybe," I said, still defiant but not half as angry as I'd

been a moment before.

"And the ones that follow, until there's no one left?" he asked. "Because you can do that. You certainly have the power." He paused, let it sink in. "You can kill them or take their memories and leave them vegetables, maybe even keep that going until the whole world is nothing, but—"

"I'd be Sovereign if I did," I cut him off, finally looking up. "That's what you're saying."

He smiled, and he looked so different without the beard or the hair, almost not even like my brother—except for the smile. That was the anchor that reminded me who he was. "You're twenty-three years old and you've got power like a goddess, like no one outside of a comic book writer or CGI guru could have imagined just a few years ago. I'm just saying … look at what you've wrought, and if you don't like it … change." He straightened up in his seat, and this time he looked pained for a different reason than physical pain. "Do things differently this time you've been wronged. Because you can choose to. That's your real power."

I smiled, faintly. "I don't have to be death anymore?" I was joking, but only very thinly, and I did it in a way that still hurt me inside all the while.

"Nah," he said, smiling. "I mean, you could just start with crippling the bastards and work up to it if they keep resisting."

I laughed, but it was almost like there was a sob hidden beneath it. "Wouldn't hurt to try, I guess." Unless it did. Unless not wiping them out resulted in another Scott, another Jamal, people who got hurt because I didn't have the guts to just drop in the middle of the Clary house and go off like a nuclear bomb.

Nuke 'em from orbit, Bastian said, and now he was kidding.

It's the only way to be sure, Gavrikov said, finishing the quote and surprising us all in the process.

You can do it, Zack said. *Uh, not the nuking thing. The other. The different approach and all that.*

"Okay," I said, strangely reassured. "This time ... we do things differently." And I looked my brother in the eye and took heart in his smile, hoping that maybe this time we'd get it right, and banished the rest of the arguments in my head for another time.

32.

Ma

"You sure this is gonna work?" Simmons asked nervously as they drove up Interstate 35. The boy looked skittish, there wasn't any doubt about that, like he'd shake in his seat, like she'd have to clean up the cloth once he got out.

Ma looked at him as best as she could, with his head and body part of the way twisted around in the van, his little beanie cap pulled down around his ears, because he was cold, bless his little heart, and she didn't let on any hint of the doubt she felt. "It'll be fine, darlin'," she said. "You're gonna get your moment to shine, don't you worry about it."

"I just want to go," Simmons said plaintively, and she knew he was speaking the truth.

"You think she's just gonna let you walk away from this?" Denise asked, slapping him on the shoulder from her place next to Ma in the back. Simmons flinched at the strength of her blow, and Denise leaned back, looking satisfied. "Long as she's breathing, sweetcheeks, you are always gonna be looking over your shoulder."

"She's right," Ma said, piling on, but gently. "Sienna Nealon is a dog with a mean streak. She gets a taste of your flank steak, she ain't gonna quit until she gets the filet mignon, either kills you or serves you up to that prison." Ma smacked her lips. "You want to go back to that jail? Sit in a cell next to your girlfriend?"

"No," Simmons said, blanching at the mere mention.

"Course you don't," Ma said. "You want to breathe the free air, go and find you some girls, not have to worry about getting chased down and beat up in a subway tunnel. Denise is right; only one way out now."

Simmons fell into silence, which was fine. They were a little caravan right now, her van followed by Blimpy's pickup truck. They had the ideas all right, were clear on the plan. They'd let Buck steal a fresh license plate in Council Bluffs to smoke Nealon's electronic-watching friends off the trail. Blimpy even had a little surprise in mind for the big moment itself. Ma hadn't ever been much for battles, but she knew picking the right ground to fight on was a big part of winning, and she'd picked the ground herself. Well, with some unwitting help from Cassidy, anyway.

"We're going right into it, aren't we?" Junior said from his place behind the wheel. The boy was having trouble keeping from twitching, he was so excited. "Gonna hit her right where it hurts."

"Doubt she'll see it coming if we can pull it off right," Ma agreed. She didn't feel a need to smile, though. This thing they were going to do … there'd be plenty of time for celebrating afterward.

33.

Sienna

The door to my quarters was still busted up. I thought about co-opting Augustus's quarters, but didn't. He was on his way back in any case, along with Scott and Zollers. Jamal was safely ensconced in a hospital in Omaha for another day with a concussion, under an assumed name. Not that it mattered. With Cassidy gone, I suspected their ability to get any sort of information was restricted to that which they could successfully punch out of someone.

No, I had other suspicions about what that crew was up to. Probably no good ones, but I was preparing like mad. I had my AA-12 shotgun loaded, my backup pistols close at hand, and an old favorite ready by my bed.

Not like you, Little Doll, Wolfe said of my last item. I could tell he was being condescending because he called me "Little Doll."

"When all else fails, try something new," I said, not letting him sway me.

When they come after you like this, go after them twice as hard, Wolfe said, grumbling softly. *It's the only way.*

"Not the only way," I said, but I could feel the seeds of doubt. It certainly wasn't the way I'd done it so far. It all felt so … uncomfortable, really. I mean, once upon a time, I'd taken that auto shotgun into a safe house full of Century operatives and not spared the shells. In war, I was a warrior, and I'd done what I'd had to do to beat a world-ending threat.

Now the stakes were a bunch of people who'd completely ruined my reputation in public (with a little help from me, I'd admit), had poisoned me with intent to kill, and tried to blow up my brother/maybe tried to kill me as well. Was I not taking this seriously enough? Part of me wondered if Wolfe was right, if I was being weak.

Augustus had chided me before against battering the crap out of my enemies because he called it "punching down." But I'd been punched up by stoneskins before, and let me tell you, it wasn't like they posed zero threat. They could survive explosions, my succubus touch—hell, I could pound on them until the cows came home (more of a thing that happened in Omaha, I suspect), and they wouldn't even feel it. I'd had to trap Clyde Clary under a cargo container and drown him in order to win that fight. They were no joke, and here I was, trying to figure out ways to take it easy on them. I might have been stronger now, but I was under no illusions that I was actually invincible, in spite of what anyone else might say or think.

They meant to kill me, to bury me, to hurt me any way they could—and on two of those counts, they'd done a fair job.

Was I an idiot to think that trying to be non-lethal in my response was … naive? Or was it a measured reply to the shitstorms that they'd sent my way?

I didn't even know anymore.

Vengeance, Little Doll, Wolfe chided. *Make them pay.*

"Where does it end, Wolfe?" I asked as Dog perked up from his place on the heating vent.

When they're dead.

"That's what I thought about Clyde," I said. "It doesn't seem to have helped."

This is different, he said. *They can't keep coming forever.*

"I don't want to be the Clary family," I said numbly as Dog got up, watching me. He had to be used to me talking to myself by now. "Always looking to settle the score. I already have to look over my shoulder every day of my life. I don't need more people gunning for me."

End them, Wolfe said. *Don't be weak.*

"I'm not trying to be weak," I said. "If you think walking out there and attempting to respond without wiping them off the face of the earth in a first strike is weak, let me tell you something—it's a hell of a lot more challenging than just burning them like chicken nuggets in a microwave." What? I'm not exactly a great cook.

Foolish, Wolfe said. *Weak of will to do it this way.*

"I won't argue with the first part," I said as Dog wandered over to me. He looked like he needed a nighttime walk. "But if you test my will, I think you'll find it appropriately strong."

He backed off as I grabbed the leash from the counter and strung it onto Dog's neck. I led him out into the elevator and listened to the dinging quietly, waiting for Wolfe to make a counter-argument. We made it past the security checkpoint, manned by a lone guard reading a magazine, and out into the quiet fall night, breeze blowing lightly, a wash of stars hanging overhead, before he spoke again.

You could die. He sounded ... concerned. Probably for himself, but still.

"I take that risk every day, don't I?"

You should just wipe them out.

"I don't want to b ..." I took a breath of the cool night air. "I made myself inhuman in order to save humanity." I switched to speaking in my own head, suddenly more aware of Dog looking at me funny. *I already don't know if I can come back from that, but ... I don't want to live my entire life apart from the world because I'm not like them.*

You could be Death, he said, like it was some kind of a good thing.

"I don't want to be Death," I said, a little numbly. "I just want to be me." And I stared up at the ceiling of stars above me, feeling the chill air wrap itself around me like a frigid hug, and let the silence wash over me.

34.

Ma

Dawn found them on a back road outside Sumter, Minnesota, and they got ever closer as the minutes ticked by. Ma was watching the road signs, especially as they approached what had been Glencoe and saw how the road deviated in order to avoid the cratered wreck that used to be a town. It didn't really surprise her; she'd been talking with Cassidy when they'd steered Anselmo there, and she'd made a mental note of it. It was pretty nice ground for a fight, after all, especially if you were of a mind to do some real brawling, just let it all hang out.

And she was about ready for just that.

They pulled in and made way for Blimpy to do his thing. "How long you need?" she asked him as they all stood there, sunrise not quite up over the lip of the crater just yet.

"Pffft," Blimpy said, shivering in his overalls. "Five minutes. You go do what you gotta do, we'll be all ready when you get back."

"How you going to keep her off your tail?" Denise asked as Ma headed back to the van with Simmons and Junior.

She paused to pick at a rust spot where it had eaten through the side of the car. "She ain't going to be on us for a while. I reckon she's going to have to track us afterward. But if she gets on us before that, I'll call and let you know."

Denise raised an eyebrow at that. It made her face look longer. "You think you'll have time?"

"Fine, Simmons'll do it," Ma said, bumping Simmons as he got into the front seat. He looked nervous, like he was going to shake apart any time now. "Just relax and help them get set up." She slammed the door behind her as she got in the van. "Trouble will be along shortly."

35.

Sienna

They filed into my destroyed quarters not too long after breakfast. I felt bad, like I should have put on a spread for them or something, or maybe at least had coffee, or something other than ketchup that was probably a few months past the expiration date.

So they filed in silently, past the place where I'd just given up and pulled my door out of the entry space, propped it up against the far wall of the living room, figuring maintenance would get around to fixing it maybe when I wasn't suspended any longer. I'd put in a request but hadn't heard a peep. I didn't even really know whether we had a maintenance department at this point. Ariadne could have cut them out of the budget for all I knew.

Ariadne, unsurprisingly, was the first to show up. She had a silver travel coffee mug in hand, and the steamy smell of the contents made me want to zoom off and pick some up real quick. She was followed by Augustus, who looked a little worn and ragged but who greeted me with a nod and not much else. Unusual for him, since he wasn't really the taciturn sort.

Reed and Dr. Perugini came in a few minutes later, interrupting an awkward silence, thankfully. I still wasn't used to seeing my brother without hair, though hints of stubble were present on the top of his skull. Dr. Zollers entered moments after that, subtle and quiet, barely saying anything but making us all aware of his presence.

"Hey hey hey," J.J. said as he wandered in with a laptop under his arm. It had a face like an alien on it where the computer logo should have been, which I thought was a little weird. He just invited himself to sit down at my table and open up the laptop, and I let him because—I mean, really, I was about to ask him for a favor, so …

Scott came in last, bandaged, arm in a sling and a hobble to his step. He looked a little grey in the face and examined the crowd in my room with a jaundiced eye, like he was wondering what we were all doing there.

"Thanks for coming," I said, nervous. I know, me nervous, but yeah, I was. This was an off-the-books kind of thing, since I was suspended and like half of them weren't even agency personnel, but still … nervous. "And on such short notice, too." I'd sent out an email only a few hours earlier, sometime between two and three in the morning, wondering if I'd even get a response.

"Well, you know, there's always a ton of meetings to attend on a Saturday," Augustus said, sounding about as drained as he looked.

I blinked rapidly. "It's Saturday?"

Scott chuckled and Ariadne shook her head. A ripple of amusement made its way through the rest of them. "Ladies and gentlemen," Reed said, "my sister, the most powerful meta on the planet. Awareness—not so much one of those powers."

"It's been a busy week," I said, blushing, brushing hair behind my ears while I gathered my thoughts. "So, uh … sorry to call you in on a Saturday …"

"If it'd been a Monday," Augustus said under his breath, "I'd have been like, 'I got class!' and said nope."

"I've missed work for the last few days," Scott said back to him. "My boss would be so mad if I missed another."

"Sorry," Reed said, "you said boss, but I think you mean 'Daddy.'" He grinned at Scott, who blushed.

"What do you need, Sienna?" Ariadne asked, right back on point.

"I need your help," I said, back to being tentative again. "I think we all know what's going on right now, specifically in regards to who's been targeting me—"

"Us," Reed corrected. My train of thought ground to a halt. "These people unleashed Anselmo and then turned him loose on the agency and the city without a thought for the collateral damage. Same with poisoning you into a coma. Even if they didn't mean to kill the rest of us, they've just missed succeeding at it several times over." He folded his arms, and his lack of beard made his lonely, bare lip look extra stern when he pursed his lips. "They're not just targeting you, or if they are, their aim is awful."

"Yeah, I mean, I got my back broke and my brother got knocked out," Augustus said. "Plus we both got shot at. You know how many times we got shot at in the hood? None. Exactly none. Take a black man out to the farm in Nebraska, though, and it's BOOM BOOM, you know? Shots fired."

"Is he all right?" I asked, now even more tentative.

"He's fine," Augustus said, waving off my concern. "Looked like he was enjoying his hospital food when I left. He was talking about staying in Omaha for a while, guess he liked the town or something, you know—what he saw of it from the ambulance window. I think he has another crush on a nurse, like he's got a thing for Florence Nightingales or something—"

I cleared my throat. "Okay. So the Clary family is targeting me, and they're hitting a lot of innocent people in the process."

Dr. Perugini snorted, and when everybody looked at her, she shrugged. "I would say 'some' innocents. Not all of you could be defined that way."

"I'm an as innocent as a spring lamb," Augustus

protested.

"They have shown an unsurprising lack of concern in their efforts," Dr. Zollers said, stepping into the conversation. "It doesn't seem to matter to them who they hurt so long as they get Sienna."

"But they also wanted to protect themselves from blowback," Reed said, shaking his index finger as he made his point, "which is why they never blew the whistle on Sienna's killing of M-Squad. They did everything else they could to assassinate her character except pull out the one card that would have finished the job faster than anything."

"Being exposed like this," Zollers said, musing it over, "they might not hesitate to get as nasty as it takes. That may come out." He said the last as he was looking at me, a sly warning like only Zollers could deliver.

"I've got a presidential pardon locked in a bank vault that will insulate me from the legal consequences of that," I said, trying to keep my head high. I saw Ariadne flush out of the corner of my eye and didn't dare look at her. "As for the other ramifications of it coming out ..." I paused, feeling regret wash over me. "Well, there's nothing I can do. If it happens, it happens. I'll deal with it later."

"What do you want to do, Sienna?" Ariadne asked, a little more direct than last time, as she sat her coffee mug on the counter.

"I need help," I said again, lying at least a little. I didn't *need* help, but having help would mean I didn't have to face this family of bandits alone, that I might not have to escalate the fight immediately to Defcon 1, where I'd be forced to kill them right off. Or maybe it'd force me to in order to protect a teammate. I was shooting in the dark, but I was sick of doing so alone. "I got into this mess because I started down a road toward revenge on my own—"

"And now you want us to keep you company while you kill them all?" J.J. asked, and he sounded, uhm ... totally onboard with that.

"Uhh, no," I said, a little troubled by his tone. "I was hoping you'd help me bring them to justice."

"You've dragged in a few villains so far," Reed said, sounding a little skeptical. "All wanted or having committed some obvious crime, right?" I nodded, and he went on. "How do you think Phillips is going to react when you try and bring in the Clarys, who—so far as he knows—haven't committed any crimes?" He looked around the room. "I mean, you and I know they have, but it looks to the lawyers out there like we have no evidentiary standards. He's going to require something other than your say-so, suspended agent."

"I know," I said, nodding. "The good news is that J.J. has a little bit on these people—"

"I do?" J.J.'s eyes were wide, his lips formed into a perfect O of surprise. "I didn't find anything on them—"

"Did you keep the stuff Jamal came up with?" Augustus asked impatiently.

"Oh, yeah," J.J. nodded, back to his version of normal again. "Totally. All documented. I kept one of his programs, too, because it was soooo cool—"

"Well, that's something," Reed said, switching focus back to me. "But this is gonna rest on Phillips's judgment. Do you think he's going to be eager to see the Clarys sitting in his jail when it's your word and some computer intel that's putting them there?"

"I don't know," I said, which was the truth. "On paper, they're all petty lawbreakers 'til now. At least, that's all they've been caught doing. I'd bet they've done more, because they're pretty good at being bad—" I paused, felt a subtle vibration in my knees and wondered if my lack of sleep was finally catching up with me.

"What?" Augustus asked.

"I don't kn—" I cut myself off halfway through the thought, because that subtle vibration I thought was all in my knees became not subtle, became so strong it turned over Ariadne's coffee mug.

"Oh, shit," Reed said, his eyes on me, horrorstruck as he realized what was going on.

"Earthquake!" J.J. shrieked as the lights flashed and the room shook. "Ohmig—"

I saw in Reed's eyes that he had vaulted straight to the same page I had. This was Minnesota, not known for seismic events. A crack appeared in my ceiling and plaster dust rained down as the intensity increased and a rumble of structural protest echoed through the building.

"Simmons," I whispered, as the first chunk of the ceiling came down, hitting Scott and drawing a scream as it landed right on his wounded arm. Another fell right after, like some set being destroyed on a Hollywood picture, then another, as the roof started to cave in around us, the revenge I expected from the Clarys showing up hours early—and in a form I wouldn't have ever thought they'd have the gall to even try.

36.

Ma

"That's right," she said soothingly to Simmons. He was sweating something fierce, even in the cool Minnesota morning. His hands were extended toward the fence just in front of them, and beyond it to the buildings that were hiding on the other side of the thick woods that shielded the agency campus from view. They'd left the car behind and walked here, only a few hundred yards from where Sienna Nealon lay her pretty little head, where she called home, where she schemed and planned and—"You just keep it up, darlin', you're showing 'em who's the boss."

"It's so ... hard ..." Simmons choked out. Ma's mind ran to a natural double entendre on that one, given what she knew about the boy, but she dismissed that thought with just a little distaste. He was a filthy little shitbird, Eric Simmons, without an ounce of loyalty to anyone or anything but his own man parts. She pulled his beanie cap off, figuring if he was sweating he was probably getting warm, and she brushed the hair off his brow, mopping it up with the cloth. It stuck there like it'd been sculpted.

"You're tearing down buildings, you hear that?" Ma could hear it. There was a rumble in the distance as the earth quaked. Junior looked a little unsteady on his feet; the ground was moving around them like someone had a sheet underneath and was giving it a hard tug, maybe even attached it to a tractor and started to drive off with them still standing on top. "You're bringing her to her knees. Her friends are in there, and the walls are coming down around them." Another big bead of sweat coursed down the side of his face. She whispered in his ear, "Imagine how much you hate her, imagine what she and that brother of hers did to you—beat you, smacked you around like you were their own red-headed stepchild. Now you can bury 'em. You *are* burying them." She mopped up his temple with the hat, the fibers rough in her hand. "Just bring it all down around their ears."

Simmons drew a ragged breath, his hands swaying like the wind of a hurricane had caught them. He wouldn't last much longer, the sissy boy. She just needed to keep him at it a little more, bring down a little more hell on Sienna Nealon, take out just a few more of her allies, probably scared and alone in their little rooms in their little hideout ...

"You can't save 'em all, girl," she whispered, feeling a strange smile of satisfaction twist at her lips. "Maybe now you'll know how it feels."

37.

Sienna

I saved them all and did it in one trip.

Reed grabbed Perugini, Augustus snatched up J.J., Scott jumped over the balcony a second after Dog hopped up under his good arm, and I took hold of Ariadne and Zollers, one under each arm, and we went out the slider that Augustus helpfully created for us with his powers, shattering the window and clearing the glass as he did so. It was a well-orchestrated escape that culminated in wind, earth and water being flung around like crazy. None of us much cared, though, as we landed soft and sprinted pell-mell for open ground, out of the shadow of the dormitory building as it came collapsing down like a house of cards hit by a fit of Reed's temper. Dust billowed and covered the beautiful blue sky, blocking the sun for a moment as everyone stood in shock in a little cluster.

"Oh, wow," J.J. said, and then the parking garage went crashing down off in the distance, the top floor collapsing first and then dropping down on the next and the next until nothing but a cloud of dust bloomed out of the earth where it had stood.

"Headquarters," Ariadne said, slapping at my ribs, jarring me out of my stunned silence. "There could be people—"

I dropped her and Zollers and shot forward, already in

motion. I heard Zollers in my head: *Guards in the prison entrance, two people on the fourth floor—*

I burst into the fourth-floor windows like a wrecking ball this time, dammit, flying straight out of the conference room where I'd made my entry and swiveling my head, trying to find the survivors. Zollers voice rang again: *Phillips's office.*

I shot toward my destination and burst through the open door, rocking against the wall as ceiling tiles started to fall around me, dust clouding the air. I found Andrew Phillips standing behind his desk, unsteady on his feet, that guy in the black tactical getup with the mask shaking in front of his desk on unsteady legs. He reacted to my entry with no surprise, watching me like I was a threat all the while.

"Gotta go," I said and scooped him up without protest. He was big, like, really big, and heavy, and as I picked him up under my arm I felt him tense in a way that suggested to me that he reacted way, way faster than a normal person would have. He didn't fight me on this, though, and I lifted him over the desk and grabbed Phillips as the windows shattered all around the fourth floor, the building stressed beyond the point of being able to hold them.

I tucked Phillips under my other arm on the fly and burst out the newly shattered windows, corkscrewing away from headquarters in a mad flight path to get them clear of any building collapses. I dropped them with the others, and Phillips shouted at me. I caught it as I zoomed back toward headquarters. "The guards on the first floor!"

I got the meaning. There were guards in the prison, sure, but it was hardened against meta attack. Those people would be safe; I knew because I'd seen the blueprints. It'd take more than an earthquake to break down those walls. There was an alternate emergency exit that could only be opened from inside the prison, so they'd be able to get out, but the guards in the first floor, the checkrooms where we entered the prison—that was about to get buried under the rubble of HQ.

I swept into the lobby and shot past the two guards that were shaking at the entry to the prison room. "Get out!" I screamed as I went past, hoping they'd just flee the damned building on their own power. I didn't hold out a lot of hope, though.

I burst into the entry room, prioritizing these guards over the ones who could conceivably make it clear of the lobby on their own power before it all came down around them. Rogers blinked at me in surprise as I came crashing in, and he blinked again as I grabbed him under my arm like a puppy. I scooped up the other guy and went flying out, passing the other two laggers halfway across the lobby.

I made it just outside the portico before I dropped Rogers and the spare, and turned on a dime, reversing back toward the last two guards above ground. Wind from my momentum whipped my hair. I could hear their screams, I could hear the fourth floor collapsing, and I knew it was going to be a game of seconds.

I shot into the lobby, asking Wolfe for all he had to try and save me from falling debris. The ceiling was coming down, there was no stopping that now, and I grabbed the two guards as they were trying to jump the defunct security barricade. I hauled them out and came damned close to going supersonic. I tore out from underneath the portico and dropped them on the lawn, falling to my knees as I looked over my shoulder at headquarters, waiting for the inevitable.

HQ had seemingly frozen in its collapse; the fourth floor had fallen, but the rest of the structure was holding, even though it was shaking like a drunk's hand. I watched it for a second, wondering why it wasn't collapsing before the answer came to me: Augustus.

Zollers must have told him I was out, because suddenly it just split at the seams like someone had sliced the corners right out. The buildings broke apart, collapsing in every direction and dusting me with a wave of brown cloud so thick I couldn't see, couldn't breathe, couldn't do much more than hold up my hands and hope most of it didn't hit my pretty face. I blocked the guards with my body as best I could, and waited for the destruction to pass.

38.

Ma

She heard the buildings fall in the distance, saw the dust clouds over the boughs, heard the thunder past the trees, and her smile only broadened. She squeezed Simmons's shoulder, and he sagged, ready to collapse, his pitiful little endurance all drained out. "Well," she said through her grin, "I reckon that ought to just about do it."

39.

Sienna

I looked across the wreckage of headquarters and over to the dormitory building, the debris that marked the destruction of the place I called home, and I felt a strange calm curtain off the rage that should have been bursting out of my head.

I mean, don't get me wrong, there was rage. It was present. But it wasn't an all-consuming sort of anger, just a background feeling somewhere behind the dejection that settled in like the quiet that followed the collapse of HQ.

"Everyone get out okay?" I asked. The guards that were on the ground around me muttered. I wasn't talking to them anyway.

"Yes," Dr. Zollers called, hustling over to me at the back of a whole pack of people. Dog let out a bark as I counted everyone who had been in my quarters for the little meeting, safe and sound, covered in dust and powder, as well as Phillips and his black-clad buddy, who looked like he'd had some serious steroid problems since last we met. He was a Hercules, I realized, and I don't mean the Greek hero. "Everyone made it out okay except for the ones down in the prison tunnel. But they're safe, just trapped for the moment."

"Great," I said, coming to my feet, brushing some of the dust off my arms. Phillips looked winded, trailing a little behind everyone else. He didn't have the build of a runner.

"What the hell was that?" Phillips asked, gasping a little as he put his hands on his knees and bent nearly double.

"That," I said, "was Eric Simmons and the Clary family making a hostile visit to the edge of our campus, if I'm not much mistaken."

"How do you know it was the edge?" Augustus asked. "How do you know they didn't just roll up in here and drop their thing down? Because this?" He swept a hand around. "That's a big mess. I didn't see this Simmons dude drop any buildings when y'all were in New York."

"Because I jacked him in the jaw and knocked him out," Reed said. Man, he looked weird like this, all baldy all over. "He did derail a train before I got to him, though."

"Well, he just destroyed government property," Phillips said, pulling himself upright.

"Since he already broke out of a federal prison facility earlier this year that has pretty much nothing but life sentences," Augustus quipped, "I'm going to go out on a limb and guess that does not exactly trip the man's worry switch."

J.J. raised his hand, drawing everyone's attention. "What's a worry switch?"

"J.J.," I said warningly, tilting my head to indicate the destruction.

"Oh, yeah," he said, taking it all in. "This just keeps happening, doesn't it? Like the place is cursed or something. How many times is this, now?"

"Counting the one where she blew it up?" Ariadne asked, not looking like she'd suffered for the run. "Three, I guess."

"I only partially—" I stopped mid-defense. "Whatever. If Simmons did this, he had to have been nearby."

"Oh, yes," J.J. said, again drawing attention to himself. His computer with the alien face was still clutched under his arm, and he sat down and crossed his legs in front of him while opening it up. It glowed softly on his face in the bright light of day, which made me wonder how many kilowatt hours he had pumping through that thing under normal conditions. "Okay, coming online now ..."

"What are you doing?" Phillips sashayed his way to stand behind J.J., arms crossed and face inscrutable as he squinted at the screen. "Do you still have Wi-Fi connection?"

"Hahah, no," J.J. said, all fake mirth. "I'm on the nearest tower. 4G, baby. Give me a sec."

"While you're doing that," I muttered and flew off toward the dormitory. I soared over the green lawns, wind biting my face.

We must kill for this transgression, Little Doll, Wolfe breathed in my ear. *They need to die.*

Might I suggest a pleasant explosion? Gavrikov offered.

Cloud their minds, burn their bodies, Bjorn said. *Leave no trace.*

Bind them, kill them, Eve said.

Please don't turn into a giant dragon unless you have to, Bastian said. *It's so embarrassing.*

"I'm not gonna kill 'em," I said as I came to the rather obvious remains of my quarters, the roof all fallen down on the wreckage of the fourth floor. "I'm just gonna make 'em wish they were dead." I paused. "Unless they get too far out of line, too dangerous. Then I might actually have to make them dead."

Don't be a fool—

Dumb—

Bad strategy—

Why would you think they aren't dangerous—

Do what you need to, Zack said, drowning them all out for me. *Whatever it takes to get the job done and maintain your humanity.*

"Roger wilco," I said, pulling the biggest segment off the roof off where my bedroom used to be. What was with all this roof moving? Twice in two days; had to be some sort of personal record.

When I lifted it up and tossed it, I ignored the shattering sound it made as it landed, focusing instead on the sight of my bed, broken but still there. I saw a glimmer of light as sunlight hit the shiny metal object I'd left next to the bed, still appearing completely intact. My AA-12 shotgun looked like a total loss, though, the barrel having caught a stray piece of concrete. It was like a sign.

I brandished the old spark gun, which was my name for the model of independently powered wireless shock weapon that the Directorate had issued when it wanted to counter threats in a non-lethal fashion. It looked like it was silver-plated, a monstrosity with a giant barrel. The originals had been destroyed when Omega had blown up the Directorate, but the plans had been saved on a backup server, and Ariadne had seen fit to have a couple constructed after the war—"Just in case," I think she said.

I held it in both hands, like a shotgun with a big stock and a charge capability that'd drop an Atlas-type to the ground in shaking pain. It felt good there, like it belonged.

Stupid, Wolfe said.

Needlessly dangerous, Eve said.

They destroy your home and you don't retaliate? Bjorn asked, genuinely surprised.

"I'm not Death," I said, running fingers over the smooth metal of the barrel as I lifted back up. "I'm not the spirit of vengeance, and I'm not here to wipe out my all enemies like some old power from the days before civilization."

What are you, then? Wolfe asked.

I thought about it and couldn't come up with a great answer, so I settled for a good one. "I'm the boot that's about to kick some ass." And that was damned sure true.

40.

Ma

The van bounced along the back roads as they sped toward the ruins of Glencoe, Minnesota. "Wheeeeehaw!" Junior shouted out the window. Ma just grinned at him; that was the kind of enthusiasm she was looking for when she started this plan.

Simmons was still in the front of the van, just shaking. Looked like he'd used his powers on himself. "You gonna be all right?" she asked, brushing against his shoulder from where she sat in the back.

"I need some water," he said. He was still pale, still shaking. He'd let it all get to him, she figured, put it all into the attack, let it drain him down. His face was so white she could see the curly little hairs from his barely-there beard peeking through. It was hardly enough for a cat to lick off if she'd doused his face with milk, but it was much more pronounced now that he was so damned white.

"That was badass, I don't care what anybody says," Junior opined, turning them hard around a corner. Ma could see the empty crater of Glencoe ahead, probably only a couple miles off. "Badass. I bet she lost some friends today."

"I sure hope so," Ma said, looking out the window. She hadn't worried about that avenging angel coming down on them before, but she worried about it now. Just a few more minutes and they'd be there, and then it wouldn't matter if she came swooping down on them ... because they'd be ready for her.

41.

I landed next to J.J., who now had everyone watching over his shoulder as he fiddled with his laptop, even the guards, who looked funny cradling their M4s while completely covered in dust and dirt, like someone had just pulled them out of a sandstorm.

"What is that?" Thorsen asked, pointing at the screen.

"Google Maps?" Phillips's Hercules asked.

"Brilliant deduction, Guy Friday," Reed snarked at him. The way the Hercules glared back at him, I suspected they had a history, and not of the romantic sort. Probably.

"Looks like Mars," Augustus said, looking at the screen. He wasn't far wrong.

"Harper put a drone in the air nearby during the manhunt," J.J. said. "This is the live feed."

"Why's it still up there?" Phillips asked, his suit covered in—you guessed it—dust. Looked like someone had rolled him in wheat flour.

"Because Harper's military and you never countermanded the order you gave her," J.J. said, so matter-of-fact that he probably didn't even see Phillips's face turn into a scowl for a quarter-second. "She's probably been refueling and sending it right back up."

"Why didn't she ask for—" Phillips cut himself off

halfway through the question. I knew the answer. J.J. knew the answer. Guy Friday probably even knew the answer. It was because Harper didn't like dealing with Phillips any more than the rest of us did; she just hid it better than most. "What's the point of this?"

"It's …" J.J. squinted at the computer. "Hold on …" He zoomed the map in to show a van streaking down a back road, the lines dividing the lanes going by like laser shots across a film screen. "I'd say they're guilty of speeding. Reckless endangerment, maybe." He zoomed out again, and now I knew why Augustus had thought it looked like Mars.

They were heading straight for Glencoe, Minnesota.

"I'm about to wreck their day and their car," I said, and braced to launch myself into the sky, my spark gun in hand.

"Hold it," Phillips said, and he just asked so nice I couldn't help but stop myself.

I flipped him the bird. "Why?"

"What are you going to do?" he asked, ignoring my rude gesture.

"Bring them in," I said. "Just like the others. Why? Are you going to give me a ration of crap about how I'm suspended?"

He looked inscrutable, as usual. "No. You're going to take on the four of them alone, though?"

I rolled my head a little left and a little right, hedging. "Maybe."

"Take support," Phillips said, and he gave a nod at Reed, then Augustus. He paused as he looked at Scott, then Zollers. "Who the hell are you people again?"

"Consultants," Zollers answered.

"Hired by whom?" he asked icily.

"Me," Ariadne said, stepping up to stand between him and the team. "We needed extra muscle."

"Where'd you find that in the budget?" Phillips asked, seeming genuinely curious, or as close as he could get without showing much actual emotion.

"We suddenly have a surplus in the facilities management area," she said, casting a conspicuous look over her shoulders at HQ.

Phillips's face fell down to the ground floor, any hint of amusement now gone. "That's gonna be a deficit and you damned well know it. This is gonna cost." He took in the whole wrecked campus. "This is going to ..." He let out a sound of complete frustration and looked at Guy Friday with stern resolve. "You go with them."

"Hey, bossman, the parking garage just ate shit," Augustus said, pointing to the evidence of his statement. The topmost floor looked like it had been bent into a slanted V as it collapsed. "How are we supposed to get to this battle?"

Phillips stayed true to his inscrutable self, but reached into his pocket and fished out his keys. "Here." He tossed them to Reed. "Not exactly a Challenger, but ..."

"Oh, come on." Reed looked disgusted, which was an even weirder look on him without the eyebrows. It kinda freaked me out, to be honest. His gaze drifted along the main driveway, and there, sitting parked with the sheet metal portico draped across it, was Phillips's company car, an orange-as-soda-mixed-with-blood VW Beetle. "Really?"

"It'll get you where you're going," Phillips said, eyeing the car. "If you can get it out of there."

"Okay," I said, and looked over my little team. "Reed, Augustus, Zollers, Guy Friday, Scott—" I paused, frowning. "What a sausage fest." I shook my head. "Get to your ride, boys. Let's go." And I started into the air, ready to wreak some havoc.

42.

Following the orange beetle meant my progress was frustratingly slow. I wanted to zip ahead with my spark gun and started raining down some lightning from the heavens. The smallest part of me regretted that I didn't have lightning powers, because I still kinda wanted those, but the spark gun would have to do for now.

The wind was cool, the breath of autumn in the air. It hadn't even been that long since the State Fair, but it was already here, lurching into the close of another year. Pretty soon the ground would be covered with snow, and I'd have to wear a coat or set myself on fire just to tolerate flying through this crap.

Or not. My base did just get destroyed, after all. I eyed the fields of the Minnesota landscape, caught a glimpse of one of those ten thousand lakes we were known for. I could just call it a wash, pull up stakes and go elsewhere. They'd just brought my home down around my ears again, and it felt like a little bit of a signal to me that maybe I was getting a little too rooted for my own good.

For the first almost eighteen years of my life I'd essentially lived in the same house and never come out. Then I'd attached myself to an organization headquartered in the exact same place as I lived now, serving a non-governmental agency until the real government came in and took over. Somewhere between, I'd chased vengeance on my own accord for a while, and it had been the most disruptive, destructive time of my life.

No more.

No strings, Zack said. *Nothing keeping you here.*

"I still have a house," I said as the orange beetle wended its way along the lane below like a bug crawling across a floor. Oh, so slow. Step on it, Reed.

Houses sell, Zack said.

"I still have a job," I said and felt a quiver. "Apparently. For now."

You can always get a new one.

I took a breath. "This is all I've ever known."

And until you stepped outside on a cold winter day, the inside of your house was all you'd ever known.

That was the truth.

The crater that had been Glencoe loomed large in front of me. It didn't look quite like another planet from here, but close. Green spots sprouted within, hints of new life forming where a scourging fire had burned that town from the map only a few years earlier. I saw a van parked in the crater, and another just beyond. Chain-link fencing bracketed the whole crater, like someone from the government had just come in and shut the whole place off on the theory some kid would get hurt if they didn't. Which was hard to understand, because from where I hovered, the walls of the crater sloped at less than a fifteen degree angle down to the epicenter of the blast where Aleksandr Gavrikov, that ass—I turned my irritation toward him, and he bore it with something like a GULP! inside me—had blown the place up.

It was an easy slope to drive, as evidenced by the cars parked down toward the middle of the crater. Ground zero was probably fifteen to twenty feet below the level of everything else, the earth displaced where Gavrikov had blasted it out in every direction with both heat and force. Clumps of glass shone in the morning light where it had gotten intense enough in places to melt sand.

I decreased altitude so I could come up even with Reed's window. He glanced out at me and then rolled it down, the wind roaring in both our ears. "I'm flying ahead," I said. "You've got a straight shot—you'll catch up in about two minutes."

"What the hell?" he asked, not keeping his eyes on the road, the baldy weirdo. "You want to have a chitchat before we show up or something?"

"You know me," I said, "I like to talk them to death before they get a chance to get too wound up." I brandished the spark gun and then glanced into the back seat. Augustus, Guy Friday and Scott were all crammed in back there. I waved at them. Augustus waved back, pretty halfheartedly. Scott did not look pleased. I couldn't tell what Guy Friday was thinking, what with the mask and all.

I went to just below supersonic, sparing the boys in the Beetle a good rattling of ears and windowpanes as I shot skyward, preparing to drop down and surprise my enemies. I made it over the crater and hit clouds, then peered down and swept in a vertical dive sharp enough to send all the blood rushing to my brain. G forces? Not a problem.

I fell at speed, a meteor coming out of the sky behind the two vans that were parked in the crater. I had to wonder a little bit at the second one. They were both parked facing away from the crater entrance where the road led, like no one had bothered to turn them around to flee.

I had to guess that the Clarys knew I was coming. They couldn't be stupid enough to think I'd let them get away with that crap they just pulled unanswered. Then again, they'd just leveled my HQ, so odds were good they probably thought they had some lead time.

I was about to disabuse them of that notion in the sternest possible terms.

At about a thousand feet above them, I figured out who was who. Simmons was sitting in the dirt, looked a little peaked. Denise had her hair stretched around her, clearly ready for battle. Ma and Junior already had their game faces on, looking all metal and glinty in the sun.

And every single one of them was looking the wrong way.

I drifted the last hundred feet and hovered above one of the vans, bringing up the spark gun without a sound. I took aim at Denise first and gave her twenty thousand volts. She bucked and jived like she'd just gotten a wicked case of ants in her pants, then fell face-first to the ground, her hair retracting to shoulder level as she dropped.

I popped off two shots at Simmons as he was raising his head to look up to figure out what the hubbub was about. "Whaa—aaaaieeeeeeeeeeeeeeeee!" He went from normal tone of voice to a scream in 0.6, shaking in the dirt as the electrical surge ran through his muscles and probably made him crap his pants. I'd heard the spark gun had that side effect. On the weak. Which I had Simmons pegged as.

"Shit," Junior said, thumping around to face me. He stood there, looking at his sister, a little dumbstruck.

"I figured you'd bring a gun," Ma said, turning around to look at me with those metal features of hers. She was hardened steel over a kind of pudgy face, a weird contrast. Instead of looking statuesque, she looked like a designer hadn't shaved the metal properly, and it gave her a toad-like look. "Didn't know it'd be one of those prissy little Tasers."

"This sucker hurts," I said, patting the spark gun for emphasis. "When your little princess wakes up, she can tell you all about it."

Clyde Clary, Jr., snickered, waving a hand in front of his nose. "Yeah, I bet Denise'll tell us all about it."

"I was talking about Simmons, but ..." I shrugged, and Junior cackled at my jibe as I floated around to hang over them at a ninety-degree angle from where their cars were parked. I didn't want to provide them with a straight shot in case someone was hiding in the vehicles, nor give them an easy time of it in case they wired it with a bomb. This felt like a compromise. "Claudette Clary, Claude Clary, Junior ... do I even need to tell you how under arrest you are?"

"You want to read off the charges?" Ma asked, leading me to believe she was going to tack resisting arrest onto whatever list I could produce.

"I kinda just want to beat your ass into a pile of molten metal," I said. "You'd probably be doing yourself a big favor by surrendering and coming quietly, but I doubt you're going to do that, so ..."

"You get some real funny ideas about how metal works—" Junior started, but Ma held up a hand to silence him. He shut up, thank goodness.

"You know it ain't gonna be that simple, right?" Ma asked, not taking her eyes off me. Just like her boy Clyde's, her eyes didn't turn steel with the rest of her. Once upon a time, I'd taken his eye right out of his skull in a fight that had damaged the hell out of the Directorate cafeteria. I wondered if she knew that—that I knew they had a weakness.

"Simplicity isn't required," I said, still hovering above them so they had to look up at me. "If it was easy to beat your ass, lots of people would have done it by now."

"Lots of people have tried," Ma said. "No one's succeeded."

"I killed your boy," I said, just throwing that out there. "He was like you, and I didn't just beat him. I killed him." I didn't add any taunt to it at all, just made it a statement of fact. "If it comes down to it, do you want to lose your grandson the same way?"

For the first time, Ma's face went perfectly along with the steel that coated it. She looked frozen in metal, clad in iron, stiff as could be. I couldn't tell if that made her pissed, scared or just contemplative, but she didn't look away. "It ain't gonna be like that this time," she said. "You lured him into a trap when he was drunk—"

"I was near to powerless against him back then," I said, "and I killed him. You sure you want to tempt fate now that I'm the most powerful meta on the planet?"

"Pshawww," Junior said, dismissing me in roughly the same way his daddy would have. The prideful prick. "You got a sense of unearned accomplishment 'round you, girl."

"What I've got is a hell of a lot of dead people dragging along behind me," I said, and I fixed him with my stare. "Also, your word of the day toilet paper is clearly paying off, so kudos to you."

"You may have walked my boy into a trap while he was a young and stupid—" Ma said.

"Well, you're half right."

"—but I ain't either of those, and you didn't lead us here," she said, and there was no masking the sense of triumph in the way she said that. "We led you, and you followed like a bull after a red cloth. All we had to do was shake your house down around your ears, drop a ton of rock and stone on your little friends, and here you came a runnin'."

The back doors to the van nearest to me opened with a hard thump, and a man jumped out with an M249 SAW—that's Squad Automatic Weapon, a machine gun used by the Army and the Marine Corps in war zones when they wanted to make the enemy put their damned heads down and stop shooting under threat of a whole lotta bullets whizzing through the air above them. This guy had one cradled on his arm like Rambo, except he was wearing overalls and he didn't exactly have the chiseled physique. He looked kinda old, actually, but big enough to handle the SAW without dropping it, which wasn't a minor accomplishment. "Meet Cousin Blimpy," Ma said, nodding her head at him.

Another guy got out of the side door of the van with way, way too much exposed armpit for his shirt to still be considered a functional piece of clothing. "This is Blimpy's boy Buck," Ma kept on making the introductions like this was a picnic or something, "and his daughter Janice." She nodded at a woman who followed in Blimpy's (I can't believe

I just met a guy who calls himself Blimpy) wake. Ma smiled, and I knew that she'd well and truly set the trap. "And thank you for charging right in."

43.

Cousin Blimpy opened up with the SAW as I quick-drew the spark gun and blasted the nearest target – Buck, with his failure of a t-shirt – as bullets filled the air around me. Blimpy's aim was off, thankfully, probably because I was already flying to avoid his fire. I was in pure reaction mode, not wanting to get clipped by a .223 bullet. They weren't exactly huge, being the same ammo an M-16 used, but they weren't a picnic in the park on a sunny day, either, and there were a lot of them flying at me presently. The chatter of the gun was deafening, a steady ripping noise like someone was mowing a lawn right next to my ear while also chainsawing through a piece of steel.

I dove left and Cousin Blimpy sprayed. He had a smaller turn radius but I was faster; it was a race, so I dodged low as I flew, forcing him to correct up and down rather than just spin. When I made it behind his van, the gunfire stopped after I heard him chew up his side mirror and break both the driver's side window and the front windshield. If Reed's insurance wasn't picking up for car bombs, I had to believe that Cousin Blimpy was definitely going to be out more than his deductible for self-inflicted automatic weapon damage.

Idiot.

Janice was gawking at me from where she stood next to the passenger door of the van, so I pumped her full of voltage and didn't stop to watch her squirm. While I was just as fascinated as everyone else to find out what kind of meta she was, I would have been a lot happier doing so while watching her on the other side of a prison cell, where I could flood her with ten thousand gallons of energy dampening gel and watch her switch from uppity to struggling to keep her head afloat. Humility usually set in shortly thereafter. It was fun to watch.

"Get her!" Ma hectored, probably pretty uselessly. I couldn't see Cousin Blimpy, but I had to guess he wasn't so sanguine about the idea of ripping holes in his van with a machine gun while blindly trying to kill little old me. Sure, he was in for murder of a federal agent, but destroying his own property was where he drew the line.

"She's over here!" Junior shouted, like it was some big revelation where I was hiding, as if they hadn't all just seen me dive behind the damned van. The hardest thing I'd had to do in this battle so far was to keep from rolling my own eyes so hard they'd do permanent damage to the inside of my head. Meta strength and all that, you know.

I heard a whine in the distance and for about a quarter second I wondered if Cousin Blimpy had finally decided to stop screwing around and just waste me through the van with the beltfed, but like a cornfed idiot, the answer was no.

It was the Beetle, rolling through the crater at top speed, looking like a rally car way out of its damned element, like Reed was going to end up turning the damned thing over before he could reach me and be of any actual use.

"What the hell?" Junior asked, spinning around and leaving the back of his empty, metal head exposed only eight feet away. I seized on this fine opportunity by dropping the spark gun and grabbing him in a big hug and then twisting him as I flew into the air at supersonic speed.

"Whut—the—" he got out as I took him up, up and more up, about a mile, then, before he could get a solid grasp on either of my arms, I released him and gave him a good shove back toward the crater. "Your dad used to say

'Geronimo' when he did this, which I always thought was kind of racist, but—" I shrugged. He looked a little panicked, arms pinwheeling as gravity took hold of him.

I didn't stick around to see the cascade of emotions that were probably setting in on his face as he began his journey back to earth. I'm sure it would have followed Elisabeth Kübler-Ross's five stages closely, and while it would have been fun to see him try and bargain with an uncaring me before accepting he was going to slam hard into an even more uncaring earth, I had shit to do that didn't involve watching Clyde Clary, Jr., faceplant into dirt.

Blimpy had apparently decided that I'd flown off for good, because he was taking aim at the orange Beetle when I came back down. I didn't waste my time going for the spark gun; I landed on his back with all that supersonic force with a front kick right to the base of his spine. If he was going to try and kill people, I knew where I stood on the matter, especially since those were my friends in that car.

I couldn't exactly feel the compression wave run up his spine, because my nerves weren't sensitive enough to detect that sort of thing through muscle and bone and whatnot, but I did see his back ripple like an alien was snaking its way through his overalls, and his head lifted off from his body like it was launched from Cape Canaveral. I'd never really seen that before, and it was really gross. You can imagine what followed, and I dodged back, not really super excited to get covered in a geyser of his bodily fluid, and watched the remainder of his corpse topple, machine gun still clutched tightly in his dead hand.

"What the hell?!" Ma screamed, one shoulder dropped as she took in the spectacle of me hovering over the corpse of another one of her kin.

"Did you think I was fucking around here?" I asked her, all my patience for her bullshit as gone as Cousin Blimpy's head.

"I think you're dead!" she screamed, rage clearly

overcoming whatever sense she had left. "DEAD! DEAD! *DEAD!*"

Before I could respond to that, Junior came crashing back to earth, landing on her very own van and turning it into a pancake. She looked, I looked, and when the dust settled, two big old legs were sticking up in the air, steel vanishing back to flesh, and all four tires popped as the frame came to rest right on the crater's ground. "Uhhhhhhhhhhhhh ..." Junior moaned, not looking like he was going to get up real soon.

I looked at Ma, and she looked back at me, her jaw hanging open. "You were saying?" I asked coldly as the orange Beetle came to a stop a few feet away and my friends started to pile out into the brisk autumn air, the odds already tilted way in our favor.

44.

Ma

This wasn't going the way she'd planned it, not at all. Denise, Janice, Buck and Simmons were already sidelined, Junior looked to at least be out for the next few minutes, and Blimpy was dead as a damned doornail, missing his head like it had been blasted off with a fourth of July firework. Ma found herself wanting to scream at Sienna Nealon, to get a good hold of her and just squeeze the girl's head until it made a satisfying pop and she looked like Cousin Blimpy, God rest his soul.

Ma wasn't left with too many options, though. She darted a look at the approaching vehicle, a whole load of men already pouring out of it like a clown car. She saw the brother, the partner, the ex-boyfriend—how many guys did this girl have in her life? This was just unseemly. And who was the man in the black mask, looking like he was about to go for a ski?

"Quit while you're only slightly behind, Ma," Sienna said from just behind her, and Ma swiped as she came 'round, missing taking the girl's head off by only a few inches. Sienna blurred right back to where she'd been hovering before and the movement of air was enough that Ma felt it. "Nobody else has to die."

Ma could feel the steel move in lines on her face. "I think

one more person needs to, at least." She stared at Sienna, breath coming hard, nostrils flaring, and all she wanted was to smash the smug face right off her. She made to take another swipe, but Sienna dodged again, well in advance of her even getting close.

It was gonna be like this, that was obvious. Well, all right then.

Ma turned her head as she charged at the Beetle and the men surrounding it. If she couldn't make Sienna Nealon pay by taking the smug look off her face by personally crushing it … she'd just crush someone the girl cared about and watch her face fall as that someone died in front of her.

45.

Sienna

I saw what she was planning to do play across her steel face before she even started moving and … yeah, no. That was not going to happen.

She sprinted for the orange beetle, and to my surprise, Guy Friday charged out to meet her, swelling as he went. He looked like one of those inflatables that someone was blowing air into, going from an ordinary-sized guy in a black shirt to the incredible Hulk, but without shredding his clothing. I was actually kinda impressed, and was tempted to ask, "Do you lift, bro?" But it seemed like inappropriate timing.

He and Ma Clary clashed, and I have to admit, I didn't think he was going to hold as well as he did. He took a thunderous punch to the chest, hard enough to break a sternum, I would have figured, maybe chop up some ribs and make them shortribs (har har—at least I find myself funny), but he was already punching back, hitting Ma in her non-glass jaw with enough force that it sounded like bones cracked. They were probably his, I figured, until he hit her again, and again, so if he was breaking his knuckles in the process, this dude was fearsomely stupid or had a pain threshold of the sort I didn't want to mess with.

Ma came around with her feet planted and grabbed his

arm, throwing him forward in a neat little jiu-jitsu move. Guy Friday lost his balance and stumbled, staggering away as Ma resumed her run toward the car.

Augustus and Scott teamed up next, hitting her with a furious wave of dirt and water like a fire hose of the mixture was being sprayed right at her. She stuck out a hand to defray some of the impact, and it blew off her like it was being shot from a sandblaster. She leaned in and kept charging, slightly slower against the resistance.

Reed stepped up, and I caught his eye just as he added his own wind force to the spray hitting her. It was enough to break a building's facade, but it didn't stop Ma Clary in her state of rage.

But that was all right, because I was just waiting for her to remember that I was hovering behind her anyway.

Augustus, Scott and Reed ceased their attack and scattered in three different directions. Zollers stayed put, presumably because he just didn't think he needed to worry about Ma for whatever reason. Ma lurched forward with her bulky arm still extended, and it took her a second to realize she wasn't being sprayed with three of the four elements any longer. When she realized it, she blinked and removed the impromptu shield she'd thrown up in front of her eyes to find the space around the car empty save for a telepath standing there calmly, leaning against it like he was waiting for his ride.

"What the—" she said, and swung her head around, taking in the three men who had zipped off in different directions. It was like they'd planned it, except they hadn't, and it had looked like a Three Stooges moment as they all bounced off one another and the car figuring out which direction each was going to run.

"What are you thinking right now, Ma?" I asked, calm as I could be. If she broke for any of them, even Zollers, I'd have some time to react. She may have been the Woman of Steel, but she wasn't exactly golden at the moment. If I needed to, I could even do to her what I'd done to Junior, though probably less effectively since I was sure she was expecting it now. That was all right, though, because I had another plan in case of emergency.

"She's ready to kill the next one of your allies she comes across," Dr. Zollers said, and there was a mournful quality to the way he said it.

Ma's head swung around and locked on him. The message was clear: target acquired. She bolted for him, and I knew she wouldn't let the car get in the way. Her steel-clad footsteps thundered against the ground with the fury of a piston pounding a steel support into the earth on a construction site. She had about ten yards to get to him.

And I had ten yards to stop her.

Dr. Zollers just stayed there, content to let it all play out.

"I'm gonna make you pay!" Ma Clary shouted, clearly pissed beyond pissed that she'd gotten so damned thwarted. She'd walked me right into her ambush at a time when I should have been blinded with rage, and here I was, cool as a winter's day while she'd had the picnic tables turned right over on her, a big bowl of egg salad on her face.

But hey, at least she still had a face.

For a few seconds, anyway.

I shot in front of her, interposing myself between Ma and Dr. Zollers. He knew what he was doing standing there, and he knew just enough about her intentions to know what she was going to do, even without reading her mind, presumably. It was as obvious as the rage on her face.

And he knew what I needed to do, too, and he put everything right into place to make me do it.

She didn't let up when I flew in front of her, and I didn't force a clash by running into her. It wouldn't have stopped her; it would have just hurt us both. I could see the rage in her eyes, squinted and furious under steel lids, and there was no reasoning with the mind beneath them. She was going to kill, as sure as I was going to breathe, and she wouldn't let a puny punch or a simple distraction stop her.

She was going to murder Dr. Zollers simply to spite me, and there was no way to stop her save for one.

"Gavrikov," I whispered as she surged forward into the last few feet between us and Dr. Zollers. I didn't wait for the reply.

I stuck my hand out and blotted out my vision of those hateful, furious eyes and waited as my palm started to glow. A blast of fire hotter than any simple flame flew out of my fingers and superheated the air between us as it shot, unerring, into her eyes.

It didn't stop there, though. Just blinding her wouldn't do the trick, and I knew it all the way to the core of me. She'd still strike out in a rage.

No, this was something else. This was a burst of fire so intense that as it hit her eyes, which were still organic, it immediately boiled the fluid they rested in, transferring the heat through her entire socket even as the fireball continued forward. It vaporized the soft tissue upon contact, so quickly that she couldn't even feel it to scream. The flame traveled through the cavity where the ocular nerve stretched into the brain. It didn't let a little thing like spare organic tissue stop it, though, and so a burst of heat that ranged up into the four figures, Fahrenheit, wormed its way into Ma Clary's brain cavity. As much as I might have wanted to mock her and say her brain didn't exist, it did, and in less than one second it reached way-beyond-boiling temperatures, then the solid became gas and—

You know what? I'll spare you the technical detail.

Claudette "Ma" Clary died so fast she didn't even know what hit her.

Her massive steel body seized up and I gave her a kick to the chest that turned her momentum away from Dr. Zollers. The metal surfacing that coated her flesh was already disappearing, returning to skin, and what was left of her head was—well, it was gross. It wasn't quite Cousin Blimpy, but it was yuck to the max. She rolled to the side and came to a halt, facedown, thankfully, smoke rolling out from beneath her thick mane of her.

"Thank you," I said to Dr. Zollers and caught a pained look as his hands fell to his sides. I let that hang for a minute before I finished my thought. "This is why I wanted you to stay."

46.

Mopping up the mess at the crater took a while. Junior didn't wake up until after backup showed, which came in the form of local SWAT, our helicopter support with the first transport cells hooked to the belly of the Chinook, and a bevy of local cops that I could tell were wary enough of the goings-on that they had absolutely no reluctance to pull a trigger if they saw shit going sideways. They all knew about what had happened here in Glencoe, and I suspected their tolerance for rogue metas was not a thing that I'd want to test. I watched them watching our prisoners, leery as hell for good reason. Junior was the first into a transport cell, followed by Simmons. Janice, Denise and Cousin Buck had to wait until the Chinook came back. All the while, Cousin Buck looked menacingly at us. The cops and SWAT were all quiet, and there were a lot of guns pointed at those clowns.

Meanwhile, Simmons and Junior floated peacefully in their storage tanks, dreaming the dreams of the peacefully stupefied.

"Well, that went well," Reed said, easing up to me as we watched Cousin Buck scratch his head with an air of confusion.

"I killed two of them," I pointed out.

"It's a low number," he said. "I consider it a personal victory given the circumstances." I looked over, and he was smirking slightly.

"Time was, you wouldn't have found humor in this," I said, eyeing him, waiting for the other shoe to drop. I figured it'd be one of Junior's boots based on the size of his feet. Looked like he was walking around on hams.

"Time was, you would have killed them all and been done with it." He made a smacking sound with his lips, and I avoided looking at him. He had a five o'clock shadow forming up his neck, all the way across his upper lip and over the top of his head. And yes, the eyebrows. It was all conspiring to freak me out. "Like I said, progress. Rome wasn't built in a day, and maybe just knowing you need to dial back the throttle a few degrees ... Especially after what they did, I think you did marvelous."

"Your insurance is covering the car, isn't it?"

"Oh, yeah." He arched his utter lack of eyebrows, and I shuddered. "All I have to pay is the deductible."

The Chinook came choppering overhead again with another pallet of two meta storage units, blowing dust everywhere as they swept low enough to drop them off about two hundred yards away. I'd ordered them to do that, because I didn't want our fugitives to think they had a chance of escape with the distraction or the dust cloud being stirred up. They didn't have a chance, after all. I could fly, and if I had to chase them down, I was going to beat them for at least a full minute, which was a lot to take from me. I told them all this, of course, and got the requisite sullen looks in return from all of them but Janice, who looked like she was still suffering from the spark gun. She was twitching randomly, and it was making her look like she had some neurological issues.

Not bad, Wolfe said.

They know who's boss, Bjorn agreed.

Whoa, whoa, I said without speaking, *don't go getting all gushy with that praise, boys.*

Tactically speaking, that was awesome, Bastian said.

A sedan came rolling to a stop about a hundred yards

away and Ariadne got out. She was still wearing what she'd worn to the meeting, but she had a Caribou coffee cup in hand now. She looked surprisingly sedate given the circumstances, surveying our prisoners as she walked up calmly. "Looks like you've got things in hand here," she said.

"Only two fatalities," I bragged, and she tried hard not to show her discomfort with that. "Hey, it's not bad considering the circumstances."

"Glad to see you netted Simmons," she said, coming to stand next to me. "Phillips is flaming mad about the campus."

"You think he's going to take the heat for it?" I asked, genuinely curious. "Or am I going to?"

"How could you?" Ariadne asked with a faint smile. "You were suspended."

I blinked. Oh, yeah. I looked over at Simmons, suspended in the liquid gel of the storage container, still unconscious. "Swing and a miss, big guy."

"Yeah, lucky we all got out," Ariadne said. She frowned. "Even your dog."

I felt a slight chill run down my spine at that. "It was a near thing," I said. "So … any idea if we're still going to be working on Monday? Cuz our headquarters is gone."

Ariadne's face fell. "I guess I'm going to have to start looking for a new place."

I shrugged. "You can stay with me for a few days if you want."

She gave me the eye. "You have a … oh, right. Your old house."

"It's remodeled and has a roof and everything," I said with a shrug. "Spare bedrooms." I looked over at Reed, who was talking with Scott. "Which is maybe going to come in handy in the next few days."

"What about them?" she asked, looking at our nice collection of prisoners. "With HQ collapsed on the prison …?"

"Gonna have to open the emergency exit," I said, running it through in my head. "Guess that's going to be the main entry for a while, until they rebuild headquarters."

She froze, taking a moment before posing the question that was hanging on all our minds. "What if they don't? Like … at all?"

I'd been considering that all morning, or at least since I'd finished cleaning up this mess. "Then that's just the way it goes," I said, and I didn't have to try too hard to be chipper about it.

47.

Moving our new guests into the prison had been surprisingly easy. Phillips had already set up the secondary entrance by the time we got back. It took some digging on Augustus's part, since the secondary entry was buried about a foot under the lawn in an isolated corner of the campus, but he had called out all hands, and we had so much security on site by the time we got back that I would have bet he didn't need to worry about a jailbreak.

We got them all down there into their new homes. Junior woke up just as we were dumping him in. He swore and swore at me, and I didn't really care all that much. He stared at me, face all distorted behind a wall of energy-absorbing liquid, and pounded on the door until the vent above him started spraying the liquid absorbent into his cell. He was back up to his neck in it in less than a second, and gasping for breath while standing on his tippytoes like a fish trying to stick its face out of the water. I left him like that; figured he'd be all set for a while.

I put Simmons in his old cell without a word of complaint from earthquake man. Him we'd actually taken the time and effort to strip down and search, and hose off since he was covered in the gel from transport. He took it all with a surprising amount of grace. Just looked like he wanted to be done, he was so pale and shaky. I'd paraded him past Cassidy, watched her thump against the cell window as he went by, eyes bulging out of her head.

He didn't even look at her, even when it was obvious she was there. She hammered ineffectually on the window until the gel came dumping down on her, too. It set off the warning klaxons in the Cube and fired off the red lights next to her cell. Simmons still didn't look, even when I paused him right in front of it so I could look in and see her trying to keep her head above the gel-line.

Janice and Denise went in with numb shock, and Cousin Buck didn't do much more than glare at us as I tossed him in one and closed the door. All told, it was a grand time, and I looked around at my old inmates, wondering what they were thinking of their new neighbors.

I mean, I didn't actually care, just was curious what went through the mind of a criminal when they saw something like that.

I stopped off at Cassidy's cell and hit the drain release. The gel that she was struggling to stay afloat in disappeared in about ten seconds down the toilet, leaving a thin coating on every surface. The autoshower sprayed the entire cell for a good twenty seconds after that, and I watched her face crumple in shock. I'm told it's cold, that autoshower.

When it finished, air circulated through to dry the place, and Cassidy was left standing there with wet hair, staring out at me like one of those sad-kitty-stuck-in-the-rain pictures you see online. I triggered the microphone. "Well," I said, "I got 'em all."

"I'm cold," she said, and her lip shivered.

"Maybe if you'd applied your genius to astrophysics or math you could have gotten a Nobel prize and a cheesy biopic about your troubled genius instead of a one-way ticket to the Not-So-Green-Mile," I said.

"Where's Ma?" she asked, rubbing her hands against her arms.

"She did not come quietly," I said, only a hint of remorse. "She tried to kill someone, so I had to put her down."

"Figures," Cassidy said, back to sullen. I pitied this girl's mother, because an angry, defiant teenager—uh, wait, scratch that. I was an angry, defiant teenager.

"I got most of them alive," I said, feeling some strange need to defend myself to this sociopath who'd never worried about the innocent people in her path when she struck out looking for vengeance. "And you know what? I managed to keep your boyfriend alive, even though he just destroyed the entire campus, so ... maybe you should be thankful for small miracles, because if I'd sent like, a SWAT team after him, he'd be dead."

There wasn't an ounce of gratitude in those eyes. "I won't be in here forever," she promised.

"Well, if the day comes you ever get out, make sure you stay well clear of me, because next time I might not be so restrained in my decency." I put my face up next to the glass and gave her a good look at the predator within. "Next time you might meet the ruthless me, the one that kills without mercy or care—especially if you do something like come after the people I care about again." She took a nervous step back from the window and I flipped off the mic and speaker and just stood there, watching her retreat until she bumped into the back of her cell.

48.

I ran into Reed climbing into the wreckage of the dormitory with Dr. Perugini urging him on. The late light of the day tinted the wreckage with a bizarre shade of red and orange like it was on fire or something. Reed looked dirty because he was, dust and grit trapped in sweat crusting his skin from his repeated dives into a very unsafe place to look for personal belongings. As he climbed out of the shattered frame of his balcony door, I just shook my head at him. "What are you doing, you idiot?"

"What?" he asked, shrugging at me. "Isabella needs her stuff."

"If you get crushed by a falling concrete support ..." I said, shaking my head. "Have you seen Dog?"

"Not lately," he said, handing Dr. Perugini a bundle of clothing that he'd had sandwiched under his arm. "Why?"

I beckoned him over and he left Perugini behind, fussing over the small pile of stuff that it looked like it had taken several trips into the wreck to retrieve. I led him off to the side, and when we were far enough away, I whispered, "Tell me something about you that nobody else knows."

"Uhhh," he said, clearly caught off guard by my request. "Umm ..."

"Quick," I said, snapping my fingers to hurry him on.

"Uhhh, okay," he said, eyes searching upward, "umm, once Isabella and I had a quickie to the Imperial March because I was afraid you'd hear us."

"UGH!" I slapped him on the shoulder. "Eww!" He flinched away. "Something that *I* would know about you—something I'd actually want to know!"

"Oh!" He pointed a finger at me. "Who came in when you woke up in London at Alpha HQ?"

"Breandan," I said sadly, remembering my terrible dreams of him only a few days earlier.

"I would also have accepted 'Hera' as an answer," Reed said, now a little down himself. He frowned at me. "What's with the weird question?"

I fixed him with a no-nonsense stare. "What's with the horrible first answer?"

"You put pressure on me," he complained. "I said the first thing that came to mind." I hesitated before speaking, and he leaned in closer to me. "What? What is it?"

I took a breath, gathering my thoughts, and then told him exactly what was on my mind.

49.

I sauntered up to J.J., who was sitting across from Dog with his laptop between them, eyeing the dog nervously. "Hey!" he said to me as I approached, my boots rustling the wet grass as the sun set behind me. "I am *so* glad to see you."

"He giving you any trouble?" I asked as Dog came over to circle my legs. I scratched his head idly.

"Ummm ... no, he's been an angel," J.J. said, voice a little strange. "I've just, uh ... been digging a little deeper into that hack of Cassidy's email and found a ... a thing ... that's worrying me ..."

"Is that so?" I asked matter of factly as J.J.'s eyes skittered nervously around. "I gotta get this guy fed." Dog barked in agreement.

"Yeah, so ... about that," J.J. started.

I anchored my eyes on the tech geek. "Is it him?"

J.J. blinked at me. "Is ... who ... him?"

I sighed that he wasn't keeping up with me. "Give me a name, J.J."

"A name for wh—" I looked down at the Dog with leading eyes, and J.J. followed my gaze. "Oh!" he said. "Owen Traverton."

Dog stiffened and froze against my leg, which gave me enough time to grab him by the back of the neck and grind his muzzle right into the ground with all my weight. "All right, Wormtail—or should I say Owen? Go human, or I will

Old Yeller you right here."

"She goes for the heartbreaking Disney reference at this moment of supreme betrayal," J.J. said, nodding sagely. "An excellent choice."

Dog yelped pitifully in what I assume was an attempt to yank at my heartstrings, but I was all done being tugged around by this asshole. "Now, Owen, or I start breaking bones in ways that won't be easy to heal, even for a skin-changing meta like you."

Dog held in place for just another second before he yipped and started to shift. His ears lowered, head elongated, his skull becoming human as the hairline receded. "Owww …" he said, and I could tell he was not happy about the pain I was inflicting with a knee right in his kidney. "How did you know?"

"You understand English a little too well," I said, "and you reacted a little too quickly to save your own ass during the earthquake. Most dogs don't jump into the arms of a stranger at a second's notice in hopes they'll be carried out the window, I don't think."

I looked at the beast that had been my pet for the last few months, my elbow in perfect position to have an accident against his spine. He'd been leaking my secrets for pay, helping to make me look like a horrible person the world over. Just a slip …

"It wasn't personal," he said, spitting in the dirt, "I needed the money."

"The battle cry of the prostitute," J.J. offered as commentary, "but will it find purchase in the rough rocks of Sienna's soul—"

"J.J., shut up," I said, giving him a good withering glare. It was becoming a habit. I switched my fury back to Owen Traverton, in all his middle-aged, skinny, alopecia glory. "You could have made it so easy. You could have grabbed the shotgun out of my closet while I was sleeping and just unloaded it until I was a bloody carcass in the sheets. Instead you injected me in the hand with—with—whatever the hell it was that put me in a coma—"

"I thought you picked up a chemical-laced flyer off your car?" J.J. asked, looking at me strangely. "Did I imagine that?"

"I don't think so," I said, staring at the man I had pinned against the ground. "I think it was this bastard right here. Wasn't it?"

"I'm sorry," he murmured into the dirt. "I didn't—I'm not that kind of—"

"Please say 'Girl,'" J.J. offered. "Because it fits really well with that whole motif I was—" I gave him the look again and he shrugged.

"P … please," Owen Traverton said as I leaned on his neck.

"Relax, Owen," I said, and jerked him to his feet, putting him in an armbar that evoked an immediate, "Ahhh!" of pain. "I'm still more human than you." I pushed him toward the entrance to the Cube. "And I think it's time for you to spend a spell in the kennel."

50.

After I dropped my not-so-faithful dog off in his new home under the earth, I came out of the Cube to find Director Andrew Phillips milling around outside with Guy Friday, the man in black's arms folded in front of him, looking only mildly muscled at the moment. "Good fight earlier," I said to him, and he nodded at me once in acknowledgment. "I do have to ask you a question, though." He braced for it like he knew me. "What happens if he forgets the safeword?" I chucked a thumb at Phillips.

My boss was not amused. "Who'd you just take down?"

"My dog," I said, my own amusement going by the wayside. "Turns out he was a skin-changer working for Cassidy and the Clary family."

Phillips didn't look impressed, either. "So he's been feeding them information on your activities, and they've been feeding that in turn to the press."

I made a face. "Looks that way. He also poisoned me."

Phillips looked at the prison entrance, which was really just like a ramp leading into the ground at this point. "He's still breathing."

"I noticed that, too," I said, nodding sagely. "Will wonders ever cease?"

Phillips stared at me for a minute without speaking. "This is a disaster, you realize."

"Tell me about it, that bastard has been watching me

undress for months—"

"I meant from the government angle," Phillips said, apparently unconcerned for my modesty. I wasn't all that concerned about it at this point, either, given how lost a cause it seemed, but it was a funny way to avoid the obvious. "Washington's furious."

"The whole city, all at once?" I didn't take it too seriously. "That's an impressive level of conformity." He let his head sag sideways in obvious disappointment. "I'm sure they'll find some way to take out their anger on me, and if it means I'm out of a job, then ..." I shrugged. "Oh, well." I looked over his shoulder at Guy Friday. "Looks like you've got your own team forming, one that'll probably listen to orders way better than me anyway."

His eyes narrowed. "You telling me you don't care?"

"I'm telling you ..." I sighed. "I'm not oblivious to how things look to the outside world, Director. I understand the political realities that President Harmon is dealing with over the next ... what, eight weeks 'til election?" I shrugged again. "I've done the best I can in the job I have. If he doesn't like the work I did, I'll leave, no questions asked. He can even trash me on the way out if he needs to in order to spare himself the poll hit, and I won't fight it. I'm gonna be okay, even if I don't end up working here anymore." I felt a surprising calm about that. It was a new thing for me. "But if he wants to keep me in this job, the president shouldn't expect anything less from me than relentlessly hounding criminals until they're sitting down there." I pointed back at the ramp to the Cube. "Because for as long as I am here, I will not quit until they stop popping their ugly little heads up and I've popped them all."

"Like a Whack-a-Mole game," Guy Friday said, nodding sagely, drawing a look from both Phillips and me.

"Yes, like Whack-a-Mole," I said, "except a Whack-a-Meta-Criminal."

Phillips fixed me with a stare. "You sure you want to

adopt that position? Seems like it hasn't worked out all that well for you thus far, being this … inflexible."

"I'm sorry if you end up having to deal with blowback," I said, shrugging again. It's all I had. "This isn't Tiddlywinks—"

"It's Whack-A-Mole," Guy Friday said, still nodding seriously, like it was go time on a nuclear threat or something.

"Uhhh … okay," I said. "It's not a game, is my point … those people in that crater would have been more than happy not letting me walk out alive."

"Okay," Phillips said, and I got the feeling that our conversation was over by the dismissive way he turned from me. "I'll let you know where we land." With a last nod, he headed off. Guy Friday followed behind after giving me a nod of his own that I couldn't help but frown at. Was it mutual respect? Something more predatory? And what was with that dude and Whack-a-Mole?

"Hey," Ariadne called from over my shoulder, and I turned to find her there with a dusty bag hanging from her shoulder. "Ready to go?"

I let my eyes sweep the wreckage of the campus, and I caught sight of Dr. Zollers talking with J.J., who had his laptop folded underneath his arm, Reed and Dr. Perugini walking side by side, Augustus standing off on his own shaking his head, and Scott …

Scott was staring off into the distance near the ruins of HQ, his arm still in a sling.

"Yeah," I said, nodding to Ariadne. "Get everyone together. I'll see you there." And I lifted off the ground, taking to the skies to race them to our destination.

51.

There was a party going on upstairs, the movement of feet on the wooden floors causing creaking in the basement where I stood on a canvas mat, staring at the darkest corner where something still hid in the shadows. The whole place smelled musty, and I made a mental note to open the egress windows before fall passed into winter and they got covered over with snow.

"So that's the much-vaunted box," Dr. Zollers said, his feet causing the wooden stairs to groan as he left the party behind to come down to me. I hadn't planned to be down here for nearly so long as I had, but I got ... distracted.

"Yeah," I said, breaking away from my quiet vigil to look at him as he paused on the landing. "I keep meaning to have it hauled off, but ... uh ... well, there's logistical concerns, and also ... I don't know anyone who carts away personal prisons. Feels like the DAV probably wouldn't accept it as a donation."

"You could pull it apart and haul it off to a junkyard as scrap if you were serious about getting rid of it," he said, easing his way down the last few stairs.

I turned back to look at the imposing steel structure in the corner. "Maybe I'm not that serious about getting rid of it, then." I paused and felt his presence behind me, breathing in the faint light of the single bulb overhead. "Is that weird?"

"We often keep touchstones of our traumas," he said.

"Occasionally gunshot survivors keep the bullet that nearly killed them. This is perhaps a little unique in the annals of hanging onto your past, but not so dramatically out of line that I can't imagine it." He gave that a moment's pause. "Do you want to talk about it?"

"The distant past?" I stared at the box, the door slightly open, the darkness within beckoning me forward. "Not really." I felt no compulsion to go inside. "The recent past? Maybe a little more."

"What did you want to talk about from the recent past?" Zollers asked, like he didn't already know.

"I became inhuman to save humanity," I said. "Until today ... I really worried I couldn't come back from that."

"But now you know you can," he said. "Does that mean you'll be okay with going down that road again? Shutting yourself off from everybody?"

"Well, I could conceivably live an awfully long time, so I probably shouldn't say 'never' ..." I took a breath of the cool basement air. "But I hope not. I carried that burden alone so others didn't have to make those choices, didn't have to do ..." the air rushed out of me, "... didn't have to do what I did. I thought carrying it all alone, being hard, being willing to do whatever it took no matter what ... I thought that meant I couldn't be part of humanity anymore."

"Tough way to live."

"I don't think I was really living," I said. "I just ... figured I'd suffered enough that I could barely feel it anymore, so why not take on a little more?" The thought of all the different gossip rags, the little leaks, the nasty stories that I thought shouldn't have hurt my big girl feelings but somehow did ... they all drifted across my mind. "I felt like everything I'd been through with the war, with Winter ... I didn't think being hated would ... hurt so much. That being alone would be so ..." I stared at the box. "I mean, it wasn't like I've been really alone these last few months, not like I was when ..." I waved my hand at the object in the corner.

"Human beings are not composed of indestructible metals," Zollers said, and now he was at my shoulder. "Not even the Clarys, as you proved for yourself today. We all have our limits, and I'd say over the last few years, you found yours."

"And here I thought I had no limits," I whispered quietly. I smiled at him faintly, patently falsely. "Do you think it's going to get any easier?"

He put an arm around my shoulder, a half hug, and just like that, I actually felt ... better. "There's a whole house full of people having a celebratory party up there because you captured and stopped people that fully intended to kill you." I looked over at his eyes, and they were warm, kind, and inviting—in short, everything this basement wasn't. "You don't have to be alone in this anymore." He smiled. "Come back to humanity, Sienna. Join your friends ... which includes me."

"So you're still staying?" I asked.

"I'm thinking about getting my medical license reinstated," he said, guiding me back toward the stairs. "Maybe open up a practice here in the Cities. What do you think?"

"I think you've got at least one client to start with," I said as the door to the basement opened wide as we came to the landing. Augustus was standing there, looming in the frame. "Hey," I said, "how's it going?"

"I'm gonna head home for the weekend," he said as Zollers and I emerged out of the basement's gloomy dark, "if that's cool with you?"

"Fine by me," I said. "Just make sure you're back for class on Monday."

He gave me the eyebrow. "You sure we're still gonna be ... uh ... getting funding for that?"

I lowered my voice and smiled conspiratorially. "When Ariadne and I set up your scholarship, we put aside all four years of tuition in a separate account, and she wrote it up as a liability on the books. The agency could go bankrupt, and your college is still paid for."

"Damn," he said in mild admiration. "I thought—"

"I take care of my friends," I said, "as best I can."

He smiled. "See you on Monday." He looked around. "Is this the office now? Because you're gonna need more chairs."

I punched him lightly on the shoulder without letting Zollers's arm slip from my own. "See you Monday, Augustus." I watched him head for the door with a trace of regret that he wasn't hanging around with us.

"Heeeeey!" Reed called as we entered the living room. He was on the couch with Dr. Perugini, and they both had plastic cups in hand—my finest glassware.

I looked around to see Ariadne sitting on the arm of one of the chairs with a cup of her own filled with—smelled like wine, actually. Good bouquet, though I wasn't really into that sort of thing. Scott was in the chair, his sling off but his arm at a funny angle, and he was looking around. "Nice place, Sienna," he said mildly.

"At some point you're going to have to talk to him about that," Zollers whispered in my ear, so low I knew only I could hear it. "But not tonight." I caught his smile, and on that we both agreed.

"You need one of these," Reed said, getting up and shuffling over to me and Zollers with cups of our own. I caught a sniff of the contents, and they were not wine. They were stronger. Much stronger. "I feel like after today, we should all be doing shots, but ..."

"But instead you figured antifreeze mixed with Everclear would do the trick?" I held the cup up and pretended to blanch at the smell. I didn't have to pretend much. "What is this?"

"It's what you had on hand," Ariadne said, clutching her cup of wine like it was a life preserver and she was in an ocean without a shore in sight. "I, uh ... stopped off and got a bottle of my own, which you are more than welcome to a glass of."

"Noooo," Reed said, shaking his head. "Drink with us, Sienna."

"Yeah," Scott said, smiling faintly, looking a little more lively now, "drink with us."

I stared into the cup. "After today, you're right—I need this."

"It was a tough fight," Reed agreed.

"I was talking about that Imperial March story." I caught his eye and he blushed and looked at Dr. Perugini, whose head sank in clear embarrassment. He smiled and I returned it as his head came back up. "No, you will not live that one down, not ever," I answered his question before he even asked.

"This is cozy," Ariadne said, tipping back her glass. "Kinda ... homey and whatnot." She sighed, looking uncomfortable about where she sat in more ways than one. "Still ... are we going to talk about it?"

"Talk about what?" Reed asked, already pouring himself another cup from the menagerie of old bottles laid out on the counter. I frowned as I looked at them; those had to be from my mother's day, and not one of them looked newer than the early aughts.

"Tomorrow," Ariadne said.

"Tomorrow is Sunday," Dr. Perugini said. "Nothing happens on Sunday."

"Monday, then," Ariadne said.

"Not tonight," I said, brandishing my cup and smiling as I looked at my friends, surrounding me here, in this, my home. "Trouble's already eaten a fair bite out of today. Let's worry about tomorrow—or the day after—when it rolls around."

"I'll drink to that," Reed said, and raised his cup. "To the day after tomorrow!" His movement was mirrored by our little circle, one after another. It was warm here, the smell of strong booze was in the air and in my glass, there were friends all around, and it didn't matter what came on Monday, not anymore. I'd find my way.

"To the day after tomorrow," I said, and I tipped back my cup.

Epilogue

The White House
Washington, D.C.

President Gerard Harmon didn't go by his full first name to the people who knew him. It was too formal, the name Gerard, so he'd gone by Gerry for years. He didn't prefer the nickname, but he knew that others did, that it softened his edges, made voters feel he was a little more homespun than his record suggested. He'd been elected to the Senate from the state of Massachusetts on multiple occasions before serving as their governor for two full terms. It had all been planned out well in advance, of course. Every step of his public life had been, really. A lifetime of service that most people would have thought would culminate in him holding an office first held by John Hancock himself.

He'd defied expectations on that one, though, and gotten himself re-elected president after beating out the Governor of Kansas in a wide-open race almost four years earlier. It had come down to the wire, really, but his taking over the post after a two-year stint as VP had given him the inside track and a narrow victory, which were advantages he was completely comfortable with. He also hadn't been upset when a pitched meta battle had burned much of western Kansas. It had made such for such lovely attack ads in the general election. How could the man possibly govern the country when his own state was burning?

Now Gerry Harmon was content to get his last term in place so he could go out at the top of the historical record: more time as President of the United States than anyone else in recent memory, clocking in damnably close to the new theoretical maximum of ten years. Cable news had been beating the drum on that one for months now, talking up the historical nature of it all. They needed something to talk about; after all, it wasn't as if these people were smart enough to come up with interesting ideas of their own. No, they had to wait and see what happened so they could choose what to report. In his view, they were lower than pond scum, but he obliged them as much as he could since they were the most useful sort of idiots.

President Harmon pursed his lips together as he gave the matter before him careful consideration. The White House Chef had prepared the most lovely French toast out of brioche for his dinner since he was doomed to work late again. He mopped up a little Vermont Maple Syrup—sent by one of the party leaders of that state, and good stuff indeed—with the last of it and ate it, careful not to drip any on his suit as he did so. It was sweet and wonderful, and he felt thankful, not for the first time, that he didn't gain weight easily. He mopped his clean-shaven upper lip and chin with the soft cloth napkin even though he knew he hadn't missed a drop, and regretted not asking his secretary to tell the chef four pieces of French toast, not three.

"You were listening, right?" his chief of staff, a woman named Amanda Brackett, asked him. She was sitting across from the desk that had been made of the timbers of an old British ship that went by the name *Resolute*. It was a long and fascinating story how it had ended up becoming a desk, and one that he'd known long before he came to sit at the old oaken monstrosity. "Gerry?" He didn't look up.

"I'm always listening," he said mildly, wadding up his napkin and tossing it onto the syrup-coated plate. That was how one did things in polite society. Both the mildness and the wadding of napkins, absolutes in his world.

"What did you think?" Brackett asked him again. Her lips were a thin, dark line, her ebony skin causing her to look a little washed out in the dimness of the lamps he'd had turned on. The office could have been brighter had he wanted it to be so, but he preferred it in this state. His eyes didn't have to work too hard to see in any case. "About the Nealon problem?"

"I know what you were talking about," he said, still mild. He couldn't recall the last time he'd actually lost his temper. It was years and years, surely. It was probably one of the reasons he won the last debate he'd been part of; his opponent got angrier and angrier and he got calmer and calmer. "I don't see Sienna Nealon as a problem."

"That campus is wrecked," Brackett said. Her lips were drawing still tighter, and he started to worry about her. More than a little, in fact. Amanda had always been a worrier, but lately, as the campaign was winding down, it was taking its toll. "Tens of millions in damage, and we just rebuilt it after that thing in January—"

"I'm aware," Harmon said, still cool about it all. "I'm sure you're already concocting a way to spin it to our advantage."

"Her unfavorables are so high, there's no way to spin it with her involved that comes out well," Brackett said, slapping a manila folder lightly on the *Resolute* desk. Harmon didn't cringe from the harsh sound, but only because he knew it was coming well in advance. "We say the agency— we still need a better name for that group—"

"Focus test something," Harmon said.

"—we say it came under terrorist attack, we look weak." She still had her fingers on the folder, and she tapped it against the blotter. "We say it was a personal grudge match, we look like things are out of control in our own house. Congress is already chomping at the bit to move this little agency back to Washington—"

"I don't have a problem with that," Harmon said. "We just kept it where it was for the budget hawks. If the other guys want to fund a new headquarters across the Potomac, let them pass it in an omnibus. I'll sign it."

Brackett made a low noise in her throat. "I can't tell whether you're actively avoiding the subject I'm trying to raise or if you simply don't see it for the issue it is." She leaned in over the desk. "The election is in less than eight weeks, and Robb Foreman is kicking your ass in the polls. Sienna Nealon is an anchor around your neck, and she has been for months."

Harmon eyed the syrupy plate, the liquid soaking into the cloth napkin. "I think you're overstating it." He added a little extra cheer; there was no need to be so down about it all.

"When you lose, do you think I'll have overstated it then?" Brackett leaned back in her seat. This was the downside of Amanda Brackett. Every once in a while, she got frustrated and it bled out. Other than that, she was a fantastic chief of staff.

"I'm not going to lose," Gerry Harmon said, straightening up in his chair and settling back. The chair was specially made, bulletproof, and surprisingly comfortable given all that went into it.

"Now you're psychic, too, huh?" Brackett asked, doing a little settling back herself. She looked guarded, and he knew that she was mentally about to write him off for being overconfident.

"I've got a home field advantage. Still, I'm not blind," he said to appease her. "I know Sienna Nealon has been something of an impediment this time around. I suppose I don't see her as the same sort of insurmountable obstacle you do, though." He got to his feet and buttoned his jacket. "She tries, give her that. Fails, makes a mess, but she tries. It's a tough job, and no one who's done it before has ever had to be in the spotlight while doing it. She's got every eye on her, and she's faced some foes this last year that would have given anyone else in that seat a hell of a black eye, at least." He took a deep breath in through his nose. "I think she could still be an advantage, and all it'd take is one really nasty meta incident without her in that job to make the press turn around on us like the ungrateful dogs they are."

"We have other contingencies," Brackett said, and there was a hint of menace in the way she said it.

"Gassing American citizens would definitely command a certain amount of attention," Harmon agreed with a tight smile. "Not of the good sort, I think, but—"

"It's non-lethal."

"From a PR perspective, it's worse than seeing a twenty-something girl beat up a handcuffed prisoner in a Manhattan restaurant," Harmon said, walking over to the window. It was thick glass, and distorted the lights on the lawn. Sometimes he wondered if that wasn't a perfect metaphor for anyone sitting in this particular seat.

"This is going to keep happening," Brackett said. "There's no reining her in."

"With a favorable break, she might just end up tossing things back our way yet. Like the Chicago meteor thing, for instance. Try leaking that."

Brackett waited a second before responding, and her voice was thick with skepticism when she did. "The media's made their minds up about her. She's nothing but a menace in their view."

It always came down to this, didn't it? "Let's change their minds."

Brackett made a deep, throaty "Hem!" noise that almost sounded like a laugh. "You ever try and change someone's mind against their will?"

He came around and smiled at her. "Every day. Hearts and minds, that's what we're here to win. Let's persuade them to take a second look."

Amanda came to her feet, and there was no doubt she wasn't exactly buying it. "What if it doesn't work?"

"If she becomes that big of a problem, we'll deal with her," President Gerard Harmon said, and he took a look out the window behind him again, and saw the light and the darkness mixing together through the distorted glass. "However we have to."

Sienna Nealon returns in

SEA CHANGE

Out of the Box
Book Seven

Coming February 17, 2016!

Author's Note

If you want to know when future books become available, take sixty seconds and sign up for my NEW RELEASE EMAIL ALERTS by visiting my website at www.robertjcrane.com. Don't let the caps lock scare you; I don't sell your information and I only send out emails when I have a new book out. The reason you should sign up for this is because I don't like to set release dates (it's this whole thing, you can find an answer on my website in the FAQ section), and even if you're following me on Facebook (robertJcrane (Author)) or Twitter (@robertJcrane), it's easy to miss my book announcements because…well, because social media is an imprecise thing.

Come join the discussion on my website: http://www.robertjcrane.com !

Cheers,
Robert J. Crane

ACKNOWLEDGMENTS

Editorial/Literary Janitorial duties performed by Sarah Barbour and Jeffrey Bryan. Final proofing was handle by Jo Evans. Any errors you see in the text, however, are the result of me rejecting changes.

The cover was masterfully designed by Karri Klawiter.

Jennifer Ellison and Alexa Medhus did the first reads on this one, so muchas gracias to them.

As always, thanks to my parents, my kids and my wife, for helping me keep things together.

Other Works by Robert J. Crane

Limitless: Out of the Box, Book 1
In the Wind: Out of the Box, Book 2
Ruthless: Out of the Box, Book 3
Grounded: Out of the Box, Book 4
Tormented: Out of the Box, Book 5
Vengeful: Out of the Box, Book 6
Sea Change: Out of the Box, Book 7* (Coming February 17, 2016!)
Painkiller: Out of the Box, Book 8* (Coming April 14, 2016!)
Masks: Out of the Box, Book 9* (Coming July 12, 2016!)

Southern Watch
Contemporary Urban Fantasy

Called: Southern Watch, Book 1
Depths: Southern Watch, Book 2
Corrupted: Southern Watch, Book 3
Unearthed: Southern Watch, Book 4
Legion: Southern Watch, Book 5* (Coming in 2016!)

* Forthcoming and subject to change

CPSIA information can be obtained
at www.ICGtesting.com
Printed in the USA
LVOW10s0914250617
539310LV00012B/318/P